Clickwhistle

BOOKS BY WILLIAM JON WATKINS

CLICKWHISTLE
THE GOD MACHINE
ECODEATH (WITH E. V. SNYDER)

Clickwhistle

by William Jon Watkins

DOUBLEDAY & COMPANY, INC.

GARDEN CITY, NEW YORK

1973

All of the characters in this book
are fictitious, and any resemblance
to actual persons, living or dead,
is purely coincidental.

ISBN: 0-385-05212-X
Library of Congress Catalog Card Number 73–83608
Copyright © 1973 by William Jon Watkins
All Rights Reserved
Printed in the United States of America
First Edition

S. F.

FOR MY MOTHER AND FATHER, WHO TAUGHT ME TO
WALK AND TALK, AND FOR SANDRA, WHO TAUGHT ME
TO STAND.

Clickwhistle

CHAPTER ONE

Dr. John Pearson sat at his desk waiting patiently for it to begin. His knowledge of what was about to happen was more an ancient genetic memory than a premonition, and he was not sure what the event was to be—at least not consciously. It was like a nightmare he did not want to remember, and even hypnosis had brought out only two things—it was of cosmic scale, and in a very profound way it would mean the end of him.

He stared at his desk waiting for it to begin. The desk was a shambles: a pile of books about dolphins written mostly by him, the tape from the Burroughs experiment that had cost him his sight for six months and his sanity for almost a year, computer readouts and statistical analyses from a current experiment in extrasensory perception, a curling snapshot of his estranged wife in a tank suit, taken at the Institute for Dolphin Research just before he had closed it.

The desk looked very much like his life, and he had no impulse to rearrange it. It was a comfortable chaos, one softened by the intuition that it would eventually seem of no great consequence to him. In eight years, he had gotten used to living alone again, mostly by living his life like a set of exercises, repetitive but necessary preparations for some undetermined ordeal.

Until that ordeal took place, everything—the death of the dolphins, the closing of the Institute, the desertion of his wife, the chemical awareness experiment and his resulting breakdown, the residual hallucinations left by the drug, even his new work in ESP—seemed as insignificant as a daydream. The events of his life seemed like tiny dots which, though meaningless in themselves, made up a photograph. Fifty-three years' worth of dots were now in place, and he waited patiently for the picture to form.

He did not hear the men enter the office, nor had he heard the almost inaudible beeps that had unlocked the combination of his door. They looked as if they could just as easily have unhinged the door physically, and he had a good idea who they were. He was not a large man, and even standing, they would have towered over him; still, he had no fear of them.

The nearest one spoke. "Dr. Pearson, His Excellency wants to see you."

He looked impassively at them for a moment and then looked away.

"Now," the second man added.

Pearson did not move. The first man drew his gun reluctantly. Pearson half suppressed a smile; whatever the ordeal was, the gun was no major part of it. The summons was. Pearson sighed and got up reluctantly. Hours before, the rest of it had already begun.

CHAPTER TWO

There were fifty of them, and not one dolphin under twelve feet. Fifty sleek torpedoes of muscle tipped with rigid beaks of bone. Five thousand teeth moving through the water at fifty knots, one hundred flukes capable of slamming a shark sideways out of their path. Fifty quick, strong bodies moving silently, like dark running ships, arching out of the water every half minute for a gulp of air and back under without the slightest hitch in formation.

Fifty bodies with a single mind, connected to another thousand minds elsewhere in the dark, vast Atlantic. All with a common memory, all with a common consciousness, all with a common dread of the battle to come. Their common mind filled with the teeth of killer whales, their common memory crowded with images.

The common memory moved to the images of Clickwhistle, of all dolphins the master poet. Elegant, rhythmical, subtle, sound and image flowed out of his mind into theirs. The common body moved to the understanding of Hummscreech, of all dolphins the great seer. Omniscient, inevitable, ineluctable, his knowledge permeated them with purpose. Diving and surfacing like the many-humped back of some incredibly large sea serpent, they swam toward an enemy even the bravest of them dreaded.

While their bodies swam inexorably toward the submarine, their minds swam in an earlier sea. They swam through Clickwhistle's memory of both their watery world and the liquid world before it. While their sleek, powerful bodies sliced through swells of deep water, they watched in their minds a calmer ocean, almost clear, in which the interface between air and water was like a separate shimmering skin, a skin like their own that pulsated with the rhythms around it, that gave and resisted as their own skin gave and resisted the pressure of the water as they swam.

As the dark, mid-ocean water slipped over their bodies, they felt and saw the clear water of that other time buoy them up while they waited for the birth of Hummscreech. They waited to defend against the teeth of sharks, and to rejoice in the ritual they had all experienced as mother or child in incarnation after incarnation. Who it was giving birth and who it was being born were never clear because they were all one mind, both mother and child and themselves all at the same time.

As their bodies arched for air and then down, they felt the body of the mother arch in the last few contractions of birth. As they felt their bodies part the waves around them, they felt the mother's body part and Hummscreech squirm tail first toward new life.

They felt a second contraction, and a third, and more and more of the long body whose consciousness they shared with Hummscreech emerged into the warm, clear water. Until finally the head slipped out with a last wriggle and the mother's body closed, complete again.

As they undulated under the waves, they felt, through Clickwhistle's mind, Hummscreech undulate toward the surface. As their own air lessened, they felt the burning necessity for air in the infant's lungs. And they felt the slow undulation of the mother as she twined slowly up after the child, urging it toward the surface and that first gasp of air that was a release and a joyous rebirth. The first gasp, which washed the last breath of the previous life from its mind and made that life part of the common store of the organism of which they were unique but inseparable.

They felt the first slap of air against Hummscreech's blowhole as the curve of his head broke the interface. They felt the first caress of the sun, and the first bright bursting through the interface into the air, and the shattering explosion of color out of the water. And then the cool yellows and blues and gray/greens of the liquid world as they sank back again, for the first time, into the quicksilver of the sea.

They felt the mother's body break the water, too, gulping air and sliding back through the interface into the blues, and green/yellows of the other world. And they felt all of the minds that made up the Self, packed off below and to one side, waiting and listening for the first supersonic trill of life.

As the fifty slid closer and closer, mile by mile, to the force from which they usually fled in terror, they felt the warm joy of the birth ritual flow through them and the same little shudder they always felt when Clickwhistle's ultrasonic melody of birth dropped suddenly into the rising/falling siren wail of terror at the approach of the Others. They shivered as they felt Clickwhistle reproduce the terrifying echoes of the herd's sonar pinging back off killer whales on all sides. They felt the grating sonar of the whales reaching out for them like rusty hooks, and they could taste the hatred and blood lust that spread toward them through the water like a dark stain.

5

CHAPTER THREE

Admiral Flushing pressed his finger against the tingling that had begun again behind his right ear. As the tiny receiver touched up against his skull, the flat, emotionless voice of the ship's computer whispered to him.

"PRIMARY EXTERNAL INSPECTION BEGUN AT 0900 HOURS. PHILLIP STUART, REPRESENTATIVE OF HIS EXCELLENCY'S COUNCIL ON SCIENCE, TAKEN ABOARD FROM MID-ATLANTIC OUTPOST NUMBER NINE."

Flushing pressed the subvocalization microphone against his Adam's apple and spoke. Although the computer would pick up his words just as well if he spoke aloud, he preferred to subvocalize. Though he had been at it for six months, speaking out loud in an empty room made him feel foolish somehow, and he avoided it whenever he could. "Have Councilman Stuart proceed to the Command Room," he said.

"AFFIRMATIVE," the voice in his head answered.

Flushing held his finger against the microphone and spoke again. No words came out and his lips did not move, but the computer heard him. "Give estimated completion time for external inspection."

"OUTPOST NINE TEAM ESTIMATES 1000 HOURS: BARRING SERIOUS MALFUNCTION."

Flushing sat back in his deep plastic chair and spun it on its spindle toward the wall screen. He pressed a stud on the arm and got a visual of the ship's position relative to the bubble of the Outpost. He pressed a second stud and the course of the *Dolphin Four* appeared like a red string across the map of the floor of the Atlantic Ocean. He studied it for the thousandth time, noting the four red areas where recent raids against WESTHEM Outposts had been made.

The official reports stated that the raids were made by EASTHEM forces, though recent border disagreements with three African SEAPACT nations made Flushing suspect them as well, allies or not. Hopefully, *Dolphin Four*, even on its shakedown cruise, would act as a deterrent to any more raids. Flushing clicked off the screen as the door to the Command Room slid open.

The man who entered looked more like an aristocrat than a scientist, and more like a barracuda than either. Flushing rose to greet him and gestured him to a second swivel chair near his own. Flushing fumbled rather stiffly through the amenities. Stuart's animosity to the Project made Flushing nervous, as did the fact that His Excellency gave more credence to his scientific advisers than his military ones.

After an interminable pause, Flushing motioned to the wall screen and said, "Shall we begin the briefing?" The Councilman nodded. "If you have any questions on the terminology or need any background information, Councilman, just press the stud marked CLARIFICATION and the screen will go into a subprogram. Just press the RETURN button to get back to the main briefing."

Stuart nodded again and turned his chair toward the viewing screen. The eyescan mechanisms on either side of the screen recorded that he was paying attention, and the briefing began. It was the standard public relations presentation upgraded with a good deal of classified material in deference to the Councilman's security clearance. Flushing groaned inwardly. Even though the computer tailored each presentation to the VIP listening, it covered the same basic information, and Flushing had already heard it more times than he wanted to.

The computer's second voice filled the room, as an actual and then a schematic view of *Dolphin Four* appeared on the screen. "*All four of the Dolphin Underwater Sonic Transports share a number of systems with their namesakes. The shape, navigation, hull, and sonar system of this unique ship were developed from the findings of Dr. John R. Pearson, the father of modern delphinology. The ship, with its seven-foot flexible fin and tapered nose even looks like the Atlantic Bottle-nosed Dolphin. The* Dolphin Four *measures 210 feet from the point of its "beak" to its flattened "tail" and offers ample room for both cargo and its crew of twenty. With its nuclear powering plant and its fully automatic support systems, the* Dolphin Four *is the most self-sufficient undersea system yet devised by man. Thanks to extensive servomechanisms connected to the main computer, one man seated in the Command Room could operate the ship at full efficiency for several days.*"

Flushing felt the tingle behind his ear and pressed the receiver against the bone of his skull again. The emotionless whisper of the computer's business voice drowned out its public relations voice for a moment.

"HATCH OPENING MECHANISM FOR MISSILE ONE SPONTANEOUSLY ACTIVATED. MISSILE ONE OUTER HATCH OPEN."

The admiral's eyebrows pressed together over his long sharp nose. He pressed the subvocalization microphone again and spoke silently. "Spontaneously?!"

"AFFIRMATIVE," the voice responded. Its other voice droned on from the viewing screen.

"Dolphin Four *is the fourth and final link in the Experimental Undersea Satellite Triggering System. . . .*"

Flushing fingered the microphone nervously. There was probably little danger in the open hatch itself, but a malfunction in the weaponry was exactly what Stuart was looking for, and although the noise of the briefing made it difficult to concentrate, he could not afford to alert Stuart by turning it off. "Override and secure hatch," he said noiselessly.

"OVERRIDE PREVIOUSLY ATTEMPTED. NEGATIVE FUNCTION."

"Deactivate hatch circuits." As long as the transparent blow-away hatch stayed closed, there would be no trouble with water, and he could leave the malfunction to the inspection team outside the hull.

"DEACTIVATION PREVIOUSLY ATTEMPTED. NEGATIVE RE-SPONSE."

There was a long silence in his head while the machine waited for his next question. Complex as it was, the machine never volunteered information. It was programmed to observe and report unless specifically commanded to cross-reference and associate. The latter two commands were sparingly given since even the probable theories and alternatives would take hours to report after the microsecond necessary to compute them. Even its summaries took half an hour. While it waited, its other voices entertained and informed the Councilman.

". . . *missiles are intended to sequentially trigger components of the Laser Satellite Defense System, which should be operational within two years. In the meantime, each missile, in addition to its own nuclear warhead which will allow it to serve as a nonescalatory retaliation, can trigger the components of our present Nuclear Satellite Defense System. In circling the globe twice before impact, it will activate . . .*"

9

The viewing screen increased its volume to reattract the Councilman's waning attention as he turned slightly in his chair and glanced suspiciously at the finger pressed against Flushing's voice box. The admiral forced a smile and the Councilman turned slowly back to the briefing.

The admiral frowned again. He knew even before he gave the command that the computer must have tried all the responses in its repertory before it had informed him of the situation. Otherwise, he would merely have been informed of the malfunction and the routine procedure that had corrected it. "Readout response programs already activated," he commanded.

The voice behind his ear responded as if it had been waiting for the question. "ROUTINE REMEDIAL PROCEDURES ONE THROUGH NINE ACTIVATED. RESPONSE NEGATIVE ON ALL PROCEDURES."

"Why the hell didn't you say that to begin with?!" he wanted to shout, but he knew it would be no good. The machine would only play back the programming which required it to answer specific questions unless asked to summarize, cross-reference, or associate. Instead he asked it for the location of all personnel outside the hull.

"TWO INSPECTION TEAMS AT POINTS FORTY-EIGHT BY FIFTEEN P & S. FIVE-MAN EXPLORATION TEAM ON TETHER ONE HUNDRED METERS SOUTHWEST OF OUTPOST, HEADING TOWARD PERSONNEL TUNNEL," said the voice, while its other voice said, ". . . *hull is coated with another discovery based on Pearson's dolphin research. This synthetic reduces drag along the ship's hull by modifying its shape to convert potential turbulence to laminar flow.*"

The Councilman pressed the CLARIFICATION stud and said, "Laminar flow." The screen paused and began a subprogram on primary hydrodynamics complete with five-color moving diagrams. Flushing had more important problems to solve.

The hatch was about a third of the way back from the snout, about fifteen feet from the head curve of the upper deck. That would put it about forty yards from the inspection teams some forty feet from the tail. "Dispatch port inspection team to hatch area," he said finally. He cursed to himself. He was anxious to be underway, and pulling the inspection team off its assignment would slow their departure considerably. They might even have to wait for a report and conference with Dolphin Project Headquarters in Port Hernandez. There was nothing left to do but wait and see, and his attention wandered back to the wall screen.

"Reduced drag allows the Dolphin Four *to maintain a speed of over one hundred knots. However, the vessel's potential speed is much greater, and speeds over four hundred knots are expected to be achieved once an echolocation device has been perfected that will allow safe operation at that speed."*

Stuart turned in his chair and frowned at Flushing. "The Council was told the speed would be virtually unlimited."

Flushing shrugged noncommittally. "Potentially, our speed *is* unlimited, Councilman. Unfortunately, our sonar isn't. Above a hundred knots, we race into an area before our sonar can completely map it, and there's too great a danger of collision."

Stuart gave a skeptical smile. "Certainly, Admiral, with the sea floor as well mapped as it is, there's no real risk of running into anything. Safe as a highway now, I understand."

The admiral nodded. "True," he said, "but the danger

of collision isn't from . . ." The tingle behind his ear began again.

"INSPECTION TEAM REPORTS NO VISIBLE MALFUNCTION IN MISSILE HATCH. HYDRAULICS AND MANUAL OVERRIDE SEEM IN ORDER. INSPECTION CONTINUING."

The admiral forced a smile. Stuart would roast him good if he knew what was going on. "Advise team: Complete visual inspection and close hatch cover with manual override. Have Outpost dispatch another inspection team to cover port-side inspection. Advise of completion."

He turned his attention again to the Councilman and paused for a second as if trying to remember where he had left off. Stuart scowled at him as if his subvocalization were a breach of protocol. "The danger is a collision with large marine life. At fifty fathoms, hitting a right whale at three hundred knots would do us severe damage. At a hundred fathoms, even a humpback whale would pop us like a bubble."

The Councilman smiled like a barracuda. "I thought the right whale had become extinct, Admiral."

"No, sir. They were an endangered species five years ago, but the moratorium on hunting and the seeding projects in mid-ocean have brought them back. Not in the thousands yet, but enough of them to make overrunning our headlights, so to speak, a danger we won't readily put this ship in."

"I'm sure the Council will approve of your caution when it comes to handling a five-billion-dollar investment," he said acidly.

Flushing was tempted to shout that if it were up to him, they'd take the risk and find out just what the *Dolphin Four* could do, but he didn't. He was under orders not to jeopardize the mission or the vessel, and he knew better than to disregard an order. Still, the Councilman's tone needled him; he made it sound as if the *Dolphin* stayed under a hundred knots because Flushing himself was afraid to take it any faster.

Certainly the plastic hull was much stronger in some ways than the old steel hulls, but sufficient impact at the right angle could shatter it like glass. The elongated snout of the ship improved its speed, but it put stresses along the first curve back toward the body that were close to the safety limits at great depth. Flushing himself had seen films of one experimental model that broke like a glass bottle when hit by a piece of wood at the equivalent of five hundred knots at two hundred fathoms.

The Councilman turned back to the view screen, and the briefing began again. Flushing nodded to himself, Stuart's missile ports were open too. When the briefing reached armaments, Stuart turned again. "Isn't two missiles rather light armament for half the Atlantic fleet?"

Flushing forced another smile. "We're not exactly half the fleet, Mr. Stuart."

Stuart shrugged. "This and *Dolphin Three* are the only underwater craft with nuclear weapons in the whole Atlantic."

"I'm afraid you overestimate us, Councilman. True, there are only two weapons systems of our class in *this* ocean, but we're only a small part of a much larger system, a sort of seagoing computer terminal."

"Five billion dollars is a high price for a seagoing computer terminal, Admiral," Stuart added without a smile.

"An expensive but necessary deterrent," the admiral countered.

"Two multiple-warhead missiles don't sound like much of a deterrent."

"Well, as the briefing pointed out, it's not the missile

itself but the systems it triggers along its trajectory that make it significant. When we launch a missile, it triggers relays in satellites and in the ground installations all along its path. By the time it impacts, it may have, depending on the provocation, triggered perhaps a thousand times its own nuclear payload. This is not your old-fashioned nuclear submarine, Councilman; this is an Undersea Satellite Triggering System."

"You forgot the word 'Experimental,'" Stuart snapped.

The admiral gave a nod of deference. "Perfectly true, Councilman—for the moment. But when we've finished this cruise, we'll join our sister ship *Dolphin Three* in the Atlantic, and with *Dolphin One* and *Two* in the Pacific, the system will be complete. We will be terminal number four in a global system."

"Your cruise is a long way from over, Admiral," Stuart added ominously.

Flushing's head tingled. "TRIGGERING MECHANISM SPONTANEOUSLY ARMED."

Flushing bit his lip to stifle the shout that almost burst from his throat, but even so, his muffled, "What?!" was loud enough to make Stuart eye him suspiciously. The admiral subvocalized. "Repeat."

The voice behind his ear said again, "TRIGGERING MECHANISM SPONTANEOUSLY ARMED."

"Trigger armed?!"

The machine repeated its message again, its tonelessness a hint that it could go on repeating the same thing forever without surprise or concern.

"Give me vocal contact with Inspection Team One." The connection was made instantaneously. "Close that hatch! Immediately! Repeat: Cease inspection. Close missile hatch immediately!" He was almost shouting now under his breath, and the screen had stopped speaking,

Stuart had turned and was glaring at the admiral. "What the hell is going on, Admiral?" His voice had the icy tone of a man who is used to being obeyed instantly. It was not a tone Flushing was used to hearing, and for an instant he almost responded to it with the truth.

"A slight malfunction in one of the hatches," he said instead. Stuart ignored Flushing's words in favor of the beads of perspiration that stood out on his forehead.

"Admiral, I am His Excellency's official representative on this mission as well as the chairman of His Excellency's Council on Science. I have Cosmic Clearance and I demand to know what's going on!"

The voice sounded in Flushing's head like the voice of doom. "WARHEAD SPONTANEOUSLY ARMED."

This time the sound escaped. "What the hell do you mean 'spontaneously armed'?"

"WARHEAD ARMED FOR CONTACT DETONATION WITHOUT MANUAL OVERRIDE OR ELECTRICAL DIRECTION FROM THIS SYSTEM." The voice might just as well have been giving the weather report.

Flushing spoke out loud. "All personnel." The computer connected him instantly with the address system implanted behind each crewman's ear. "We have a hot one in the can." His voice dropped into inaudibility again. "Direct link to Inspection Team One, two way."

Even as he talked, the computer completed his message to the crew. All over the ship, men's heads rang with the words, "CONDITION WHITE HOT. THIS IS NOT A DRILL. DEACTIVATION CREWS ASSEMBLE. ALL STATIONS SECURE AGAINST LAUNCH. CONDITION WHITE HOT. DEACTIVATION CREWS PROCEED CODE GREEN. GO IMMEDIATELY TO YOUR STATIONS." Only the men on the deactivation teams heard the rest of the message. "WARHEAD SPONTANEOUSLY ARMED. ACTIVATE MANUAL OVERRIDE IMMEDIATELY."

Stuart grabbed at Flushing's lapels, shouting, "What's going on?!"

Flushing continued to subvocalize. "Is that hatch closed yet?"

The only response he got was a mixture of screams and muffled curses. "What the hell's going on out there?" he shouted aloud. Stuart was shouting also. There was no longer any sound at all from outside.

Flushing shouted to the computer. "Sonar readout."

The toneless voice behind his ear droned again. "TWO INDECIPHERABLE READINGS ON INSPECTION TEAM. TONE RESPONSE INDICATES FIFTY TO SIXTY CETACEANS APPROXIMATELY TWELVE FEET IN LENGTH. ONE CETACEAN THIRTY FEET IN LENGTH. PROVISIONAL IDENTIFICATION: FIFTY DOLPHINS AND ONE KILLER WHALE."

"Dolphins!" Flushing shouted. "You stupid goddamned piece of junk, are you telling me we're being attacked by dolphins?!"

"ATTACK INFERENCE INDETERMINABLE. SONAR INDICATES ONLY THE PRESENCE AND FRENZIED ACTIVITY OF FIFTY MEMBERS OF SPECIES 'TURSIOPS TRUNCATUS' AND ONE MEMBER OF 'ORCINUS ORCA.' "

Stuart had him by the lapels again, his face almost touching the admiral's. With each word, he slammed handfuls of the admiral's uniform against the man's chest. "For Christ's sake, what's going on?!"

Flushing seemed to have lost all hope that anything would ever make sense again. He shook his head slowly from side to side and suppressed a laugh. Calmly he brushed Stuart's hands from his uniform. Stuart let his hands drop and stepped back. Flushing, with an insane nod of his head and a half smile said to him, "Essentially, Councilman, we are sitting less than fifty feet from an armed nuclear weapon, in a five-billion-dollar weapons system that is under attack by dolphins." Then he laughed.

Stuart stepped back, stupefied, and collapsed into his chair. Flushing slumped into his chair, still laughing. The computer had switched to its own hull microphones and was feeding him sounds from the outside. The screams of the men had ceased completely, but he could hear the clicks and shrillings of the dolphins and occasionally a high whistle like a railroad train running over his ship. Only the voice of the computer snapped him back to reality.

"DISARMING CREW REPORTS HATCH WILL NOT RESPOND TO ELECTRONIC OVERRIDE."

Flushing cut in. "Then try manu—"

"MANUAL OVERRIDE NEGATIVE FUNCTION. BLAST DOOR ALSO NEGATIVE FUNCTION."

"Then get a torch down there and cut it open!"

"SECONDARY CREW SENT FOR LASER TORCH. APPROXIMATE CUTTING TIME FOR BLAST DOOR, ONE HOUR."

"Not the door! Cut through the panel to the control circuit to the right of the door. Cut those circuits! There's only two inches of plastic there, it shouldn't take more than fifteen minutes."

"APPROXIMATE CUTTING TIME: FOURTEEN MINUTES."

Flushing groaned. "Get another torch!"

"CREW DISPATCHED FOR SECOND TORCH. CUTTING TIME APPROXIMATELY EIGHT MINUTES. MISSILE HATCH STILL OPEN. MISSILE STILL ARMED."

"Where is it aimed? Maybe we can fire it."

"PRESENT SETTING: ZERO DEGREES. DIRECTLY OVERHEAD. STRATOSPHERIC DETONATION POSSIBLE WITHOUT DAMAGE TO SATELLITES OF EITHER 'EASTHEM' OR 'SEAPACT' NATIONS IF LAUNCH IS COMPLETED WITHIN TEN MINUTES."

Flushing shouted, "Deactivation crew, keep cutting

at that panel. You'll get a thirty-second warning if we have to launch. Starboard Inspection Team, what the hell's going on out there?"

A new voice rang in Flushing's head. "Inspection of one third of hull completed, sir."

"What??!!!"

"One third of hull inspection completed, sir. No damage or malfunction visible. No signs of stress fatigue in plastic hull structure. No breaks in synthetic dermis. Estimated time of completion . . ."

"I don't care about the goddamn inspection! What's happening forward?!"

"Forward, sir?"

"All hell's breaking loose fifty yards from you and you can't hear it!"

"We were preoccupied with the inspection, sir."

"Fifty dolphins clicking and whistling like a god-damned freight train right on top of you, and you can't hear them!!"

"Sir, the stress-testing gear makes too much noise, sir."

"Well, what do you see now?"

"Nothing within our visibility range, sir."

"Well, get forward and see what the hell's going on!"

"Yessir."

Flushing slapped his forehead with the heel of his hand. "What the hell am I thinking of! Give me a visual on that hatch area, wide angle and vertical."

Stuart slumped in the chair, staring blankly at the screen. His eyes had registered on the eyescan mechanism, and the briefing had begun again. Flushing's command cleared the screen, and the multicolored diagram of the land and air nuclear weapons the dolphin's missiles would automatically trigger in its flight disappeared.

The screen filled again with a dim cloudy picture of the immediate area above the open hatch. Torpedo-shaped shadows flashed across the screen, curved outward again or streaked vertically away from the camera. Far above hung a shadow, surrounded by a number of moving shapes half its size.

"Correlate that visual with your sonar."

The response was, as always, immediate. "LARGER SHAPE APPEARS TO BE OUTSIZED 'ORCINUS ORCA,' KILLER WHALE. SMALLER, MOVING SHAPES APPEAR TO BE 'TURSIOPS TRUNCATUS,' COMMONLY KNOWN AS THE ATLANTIC, OR BOTTLE-NOSED, DOLPHIN."

"This is Rescue One. We are at the hatch area. No survivors, sir. Bodies look pretty badly mutilated too. Looks like they were attacked by something."

"What about the hatch?"

"The manual lever is all bent to hell. Looks like something big hit it. No way it's going to shut."

"Give me a visual on the hatch."

The shadowy shapes colliding in the misty water overhead disappeared, to be replaced by a large, square hole in the curving forward deck. A circle of light shone up out of it, but the top of the missile was out of sight.

The angle of vision widened to include the hatch cover which had been slid back. The men of the rescue crew could be seen floating away from the hole like huge tangles of seaweed. At the end of the hatch cover, five dolphins could be seen rooting at it with their beaks and thrashing their flukes violently.

"Can you shut it by hand? Push it?" Flushing asked.

"We can try." The four men of the rescue team moved toward the far end of the hatch cover. One, then two more, men swam into the picture from the left. All seven men swam to the edge of the cover. The dolphins backed off at their approach. All seven braced themselves as much as they could against the hull and tried to slide the hatch cover closed. They looked like grotesque spiders doing some insane arachnid dance in the shadowy water. Finally they stopped.

"No way this is going to move, sir."

A second voice, apparently from a figure swimming alongside the runners within which the hatch cover moved, added, "No good, Captain. The track's bent almost as bad as the handle of the hydraulic closing mechanism. No way we could shut this even if the circuitry was working."

Another voice cut in from elsewhere in the ship. "Wall near the blast door has been breached. Top circuitry has been disconnected. Cutting toward second circuit still in progress."

The flat voice of the computer interrupted. "TRAJECTORY MECHANISM SPONTANEOUSLY ACTIVATED."

"Jesus Christ!" Flushing groaned, "why wasn't that shut off automatically?"

"NO ORDER TO LOCK TELEMETRY RECEIVED."

Flushing knew the response would be the same even before he gave the order. "Override."

"NEGATIVE FUNCTION."

"What's the new trajectory?"

"STILL TURNING."

Overhead, the dolphins flashed and struck, flashed and struck time after time against the body and head of the killer whale, which slashed at each blow with its six-inch teeth, tearing its attackers and adding to the murkiness of the water until it was almost obscured. Even if the men below had been watching, they would not have seen the battle until the whale began to sink toward the deck.

"How much longer on that door?"

"Another two or three minutes until we get to the cable. Thirty seconds to cut it."

"How long before that satellite closes that launch window?"

"ONE MINUTE, NINE SECONDS."

Flushing closed his eyes and tried to think. If he was going to launch it, it would have to be soon. He groaned. He had forgotten that its trajectory had changed.

"What's the status of the trajectory mechanism?"

"TRAJECTORY MECHANISM HAS CEASED OPERATION SPONTANEOUSLY."

"What's the new trajectory?"

"SIX DEGREES SHORT OF PATH ONE."

"Any chance for a vertical launch?"

"NEGATIVE."

"Can you override new trajectory?" Flushing asked without hope.

"AFFIRMATIVE."

Another voice added more hope. "Door released, Captain. But it's jammed. Only the bottom half can move now that we had to cut the top cable. Wait a minute, we've got somebody trying to squeeze through."

"Override arming device."

"AFFIRMATIVE FUNCTION. MISSILE DISARMED."

Flushing breathed a sigh of relief. The dead whale floated toward the bottom.

CHAPTER FOUR

Fifty sleek bodies willed themselves toward the Mid-Atlantic Ridge. Infrequent echoes came back to them through the water, indicating a vast open space filled only with an occasional fish or small school they could not pursue. In their minds, Clickwhistle's song took them back again to the ritual of Hummscreech's birth. They felt again the echoes come back time after time with the mass and thickness and consistency that spelt killer whale. They heard the echoes of their sonar whistles ripple sideways and return in inverted parabolas from the bodies of the pack that circled them, round and round, waiting their turn.

A thousand years ahead from the event, they felt a growing terror flow through them through Clickwhistle's song. They felt the panic and heard the incessant rising/dropping scream that Clickwhistle doubled over and over behind the pictures that issued from his memory. Swimming toward their own death, some of them shivered despite the warmth of the water.

Closing to within a half mile of their enemy, they felt the terror of the surrounded herd surge into them out of the past through the medium of Clickwhistle's vivid remembering. Clickwhistle felt in return their own growing fear as they approached the spot where they knew their enemy would be, and he let it play back to them through his mediumship and worked it into the pictures and the feelings that he dredged up out of the communal past of the herd.

He let their own suppressed terror counterpoint the terror he funneled out of the past as the killer whale, ten tons of appetite, broke the circle of whales and curved toward its prey. The circle closed behind the whale like the interface closing behind the dive of a dolphin.

Clickwhistle let the picture of the two events overlap for a moment before he drove into their minds the four half rows of teeth, like spikes, and the first flash of jaws and blood as the killer whale slashed at the first dolphin, tearing him, overrunning him, and swallowing him down. The rest of the dolphins dove and fled, only to come too close to the whirling rim of murderous teeth that waited patiently for a turn and drove them back toward the same savage triangular fin that broke the interface like a sail and disappeared only when the mountain of flesh beneath it dove and tore and swallowed again.

Clickwhistle's mind fed back to the fifty their own fear as they smelled the strong urine scent of the killer whale they hunted, and with it Clickwhistle sent the terror of that past herd as whale after whale broke the circle, slashed in among them, tore and swallowed and returned to the never-ending circle. He let the taste of dolphin blood seep back to the fifty and mingled it with the taste of their own blood which they would inevitably taste before long.

He let the terror peak and with it projected pictures of row after row of curved teeth snapping together, tearing, pulling in, gouging, as the deadly wheel turned, dolphin after dolphin, until the herd had dwindled by more than half. He let them hear the young squealing inside the tiny square the mature dolphins had formed around them.

Then Clickwhistle modulated the rising/falling pitch of his whistle until it sounded like the cry of a child in terror, and over it he sent the fifty a picture of Hummscreech's newly reborn body as it passed, torn and bloody, down the throat of the whale into the soft coffin of the whale's stomach to lie rotting among the seals and larger dolphins taken in successive meals all the way up from Antarctica.

He held for them that last picture, until they arrived and were in sight of this huge killer whale that bobbed steadily over the forward hatch of the submarine, working, with the pitch of his voice and the electricity of his brain, the intricate machinery of the vessel's weaponry.

When they were within striking distance, he dissolved the picture and burst into a transmission of pure emotion. From the Self's living store in Longscreech, Clickwhistle funneled to them pure shark-like rage, so that it dwindled their own fear almost to extinction.

As they took a long last breath and curved themselves down toward their prey, he sent them the picture of that past dolphin school hemmed in, moving as one being, without hope of escape, toward the nearest of the circling whales, not to break out but merely to take with them one of their tormentors.

As they dove, picking up speed, he sent them picture after picture of the trapped dolphins and they struck, one after another, so rapidly that they seemed a single, pointed spear driving into the white underbelly of the whale, knocking it back out of the circle, pulverizing its stomach, until it dropped lifelessly away from them. He sent them echoes of the circle breaking as the whales lost their discipline and tried to make a grab at the dolphins, who had broken their circle and were all scattering into open water.

Clickwhistle

Clickwhistle's sounds trilled into the supersonic, frequency above frequency, until he reached notes no other dolphin could reach and wove them into a multistranded vision no other dolphin could articulate. Note by note, he amplified the fifty's own rage and determination as they dove one after another, like darts, into the belly of the whale.

They dove on the power of his song until they had made their first run and the present overwhelmed even Clickwhistle's poetry, and there was nothing in their minds except air and the next kamikaze dive toward the slashing jaws of the whale.

As they dove, Clickwhistle took from their minds all that was happening to them and funneled it back to the rest of the Self, which waited. Those who waited felt again the marvelous suppleness of the form they had chosen to inhabit on the new planet. Those who waited felt again the surge of battle against the ancient enemy they had fought before so many light years away that only a poet like Clickwhistle could still make the memory live.

Clickwhistle held back nothing, not the terror of Lowwhistle as he made his first pass, and the huge jaws swung toward him and closed along his side, tearing him open even before he could drive his body home like a punch. Not the pain, or the taste of dolphin blood in the mouths of those that dove after him, hitting again and again at the resilient flesh of the whale, like a tireless in-fighter punching away at a slugger. Not the way the bite tore them apart and let them drop toward the bottom like scraps.

He enveloped the mind of each of the fifty and blended them all into a picture and a sound that passed beyond words or ideas and became pure experience. No dolphin felt the snap of the six-inch teeth, but all dolphins felt them, through Clickwhistle. No hard beak collided with soft blubber at sixty knots, but all beaks felt the satisfaction of the blow. No terrifying echo reverberated closer and closer as the dive carried one of the fifty into his adversary, but all dolphins heard it and shook with terror at it. No dolphin felt the absolute necessity to turn aside at the last moment and avoid the jaws and still refused the necessity, but all dolphins felt the necessity and knew what the battle to do what it was instinctive not to do was like.

No dolphin broke the interface and paused an instant before the next dive without Clickwhistle sending into his mind a picture of Home, of the shape they had known so many incarnations ago on a place so far removed that it could no longer be imagined. No dolphin dove without Clickwhistle filling his mind with the battle that had raged between the Self and the Others in that far-off universe, a thousand eons before.

No dolphin dove for that soft belly but Clickwhistle made him see the shape that the whale had had in their lost world in a time beyond memory. None of the fifty hit the whale who did not know at the instant of impact the enemy that had pursued them across space and time to destroy them once and for all. Not one who flung himself like a twelve-foot bullet at the belly of the whale did not know past certainty that the guerrilla war they and the whales had waged against each other on this small planet was over and that they were once again joined in a battle to the death.

Every stroke was one more in the eternal battle against an implacable enemy that could be neither conquered nor evaded. Not a billion light years, not a million incarnations each, had let them escape the force that pursued them across the universe the way death pursued life, and had found them again and again. There was no place on the planet left to run to, there was no place left to hide. Their old indestructible nemesis was on them again, and the best they could hope for was to break its circle one more time and flee outward again, pursued by the organism which lived only for their destruction.

No dolphin dove toward the mammoth shape that did not know what the whale was doing with the controls of the ship beneath it. Not one hit it that did not feel the whale's grasp on the electrical fields of the vessel slip the tiniest fraction. Had it not had to tie up so much of its mind and reflexes controlling the ship below, they might never have killed it. But kill it they did, and the trill of triumph flowed back through Clickwhistle to those who waited.

Between two enormous waves of joy, Clickwhistle floated, both receiving and sending, back and forth, from those surviving twenty-five there to the rest of the Self gathered around him. Back and forth, he let the emotion of the triumph vibrate from one to the other, mingling with it a picture of Home and amplifying it with trills of his own, until seven shadows fell across it.

CHAPTER FIVE

Flushing began to relax as the reports flowed in. A voice from the missile hatch informed him, "Electric motor on here, Captain." He watched the wall screen as the hatch door moved a few inches forward and jammed against the bent track, two men scrambling clear of it just in time to keep their flippers from being caught.

"We have a man halfway in through the blast door, Captain. We expect . . ." The transmission was drowned in a scream. "Jesus Christ! The door's closing again! He's trapped! Get that torch over here. Captain, we've . . ."

The toneless voice of the computer cut in again, "MISSILE REARMED."

Flushing was on his feet squealing in disbelief.

"ALL OVERRIDES NEGATIVE FUNCTION AGAIN. TRAJECTORY CORRECTING TOWARD PATH ONE. NEW IMPACT POINT 150-11A."

"No!" Flushing's shout stuck in his throat. Path One circled the world from east to west, triggering every attack system in the Western Hemisphere and a third of those in the Eastern before it impacted on the African continent. It was the Doomsday Run. The new impact area was on the border of a SEAPACT nation and would trigger retaliation from friend and foe alike.

"DATA BANKS EMPTIED TO TERMINAL ON OUTPOST EIGHT." The computer's announcement was the equivalent of a man's last words. The voice of the computer was almost drowned out by the screams of the men near the partially opened blast door.

"IGNITION IN THE MISSILE."

On the screen, the hole in the deck came alive with light. The shadows of the rescue team could be seen scrambling over the edge of the hull out of the picture, and in the upper right-hand corner, had either Flushing or Stuart had presence of mind enough to see it, the body of the whale dropped slowly into the picture.

No one really saw the blast.

CHAPTER SIX

Only the stark terror of the four dolphins nearest the surface broke the spell as the other seven killer whales, answering the cries of their brother, dove into the pack of the victorious dolphins. Each an oversized fifteen tons, they fell on the dolphins like massive wolves. Only the ten dolphins who had accompanied their victim toward the bottom, trilling their victory over it, escaped the jaws of the pack. Like all their victories, it was only temporary, no more than a diversion that would let them escape again. The whales pulled back, forming an impenetrable circle of death around the largest of the pack, whose mind probed the vessel and picked up all the controls the dead whale had dropped.

But the ten who had followed the huge corpse toward the bottom knew instantly what had happened. Even before the creature in the body above had seized the circuitry they knew what would happen and what the end would be. As one, they swam under the sinking form or grasped it with their teeth along the fins and flukes and edged it down toward the sub. They forced it like a huge stone toward the small mouth out of which the death of their adopted planet would instantly come flying.

Too late to stop them, the whales realized what was happening and broke their circle. The fifteen tons of meat and muscle dropped over the tiny opening like a hand closing a mouth. The silver needle of death shot up the tube, slamming into the body with all the force of an impact on solid ground.

In the instant before the flash and heat of the detonation turned the sea to vapor, incinerating the sensitive velvet skins of his brothers, Clickwhistle sent them a last picture of the vast, dead sea of space, and the liquid world from which they had come so long before.

Clickwhistle held the picture long after there was no mind left to receive it. Alone, he carried the sensation of charring skin transmitted by the minds of the perished dolphin warriors. He alone felt so many of his kind turn to ash within the circle of the fireball that foamed upward like the sea retching.

Even the knowledge that seven of the enemy had ceased forever to exist did not ease the pain Clickwhistle felt, and refused to pass on. All he transmitted back to the rest was the last trill of triumph as the body of the dead whale slammed into the missile port, blocking it just in time. There would be time enough to let them know that the long battle for earth had just begun.

CHAPTER SEVEN

Dr. Pearson walked down the corridor between his guards like a leprechaun captured by giants. He had given no resistance and the guards had relaxed. A second set of guards halted them at the door of the conference room and checked Pearson's voiceprint on a portable unit. His own guards opened the door for him and ushered him inside.

He recognized the men around the oval table as the most important and powerful men in the Hemispheric Government. Most of the faces were familiar to him; at one time or another he had either gone to them for funds or met them at one briefing or another for His Excellency.

His Excellency looked up at him with expressionless eyes and then smiled. It was a thoroughly convincing smile, and Pearson had fallen for it before. Even the ruthlessness of the eyes could not deny its warmth. His Excellency nodded him to an empty chair halfway around the table and waited until he had seated himself before he spoke.

"*Dolphin Four* is dead," was all he said.

A disdainful smile played across the leprechaun face. It was the kind of quote that gave a man a place in history if he were lucky enough to have said it at some major milestone in the development of a culture, as His Excellency was well aware. He had chosen the words carefully, and everyone in the room knew it. Only Pearson had the temerity not to take it at face value.

"Did you have me abducted just to play straight man, Your Excellency?" Pearson answered.

The table stiffened as one man; the warmth went out of His Excellency's smile. It was not the first time His Excellency had had to have a remark of Pearson's edited from the historical record, and he chalked up another minor debt against the psychophysiologist in his private, mental book of the damned.

But His Excellency was not a man to get angry. He went on as if nothing untoward had been said. "You've carried out a lot of experiments with dolphins, Doctor." Pearson winced; the eye of the dying dolphin floated before him for an instant. He could never remember whether it had been the second or the fourth that had looked at him in that pitying, reproachful way, but it was a look that never left him. "We need your knowledge," His Excellency went on.

Pearson shook his head. "I haven't worked with a dolphin in eight years. I'm not qualified any more."

His Excellency smiled at him like an accomplice. "You're too modest, Doctor. No man alive has greater knowledge of dolphins than you. The *Dolphin* Series could never have been built without your research. WESTHEM would be practically defenseless without your work."

"I worked with *dolphins*, not ships or weapons!" he said bitterly.

His Excellency shrugged, the Judas smile was back. "Perhaps," he said, "but the weapons system would not work without the vessels your discoveries helped create." Pearson winced again. His Excellency went on. "Of course, many of the men around this table must share

33

the credit for financing your research." The subtle hint of his complicity in the use of his research did not escape Pearson. Once he had thought that the access it had given him to the seats of power would allow him to control its use. He had been naive then, but that had been a long time before.

"I'll remember that for the war crimes trials," he said.

A bulldog man standing almost invisibly behind His Excellency's chair thrust himself forward. "Dr. Pearson," he rasped, "are you aware of the penalty for treason?"

"About as aware as you are of the penalty for genocide, Mr. Kirby."

His Excellency waved Kirby back into place with the back of his fingers. The smile had gone ice cold. In an instant it was gone completely and the face was as expressionless as the eyes. Pearson waited for the trap to spring. His Excellency touched a stud on the arm of his chair and the room filled with sound.

"This data was transmitted to Outpost Eight by *Dolphin Four* in accordance with the Imminent Destruction Procedures authorized by His Excellency's High Command. Instantaneous transfer of system's memory was incomplete. Transmission was interrupted by electrical field disturbance. Transmission was intermittent and Perry wave distortion prevented reproduction of visual data."

The voice stopped and the first exchange between Flushing and the computer began.

When the transcription had degenerated into the crackling of vaporized equipment, His Excellency looked at Pearson. Pearson shook his head incredulously. "You can't seriously believe that dolphins blew up a nuclear submarine."

His Excellency glared at Pearson for a moment before answering and weighed the necessity of having the remark edited. Even without the tone of sarcasm, it was too preposterous to be anything else. "We believe, Dr. Pearson," he answered sternly, "that whatever force was used to seize the weapons systems of the *Dolphin Four* caused nearby dolphins to go berserk. You are to determine what kind of force could produce that effect. Once we know what the force is, we're one step toward finding out who used it and two steps toward defending against it."

His Excellency spoke to Kirby without taking his eyes off Pearson. "See that Dr. Pearson gets a copy of the transmission to analyze on his flight down."

Pearson cocked his head in an unasked question. His Excellency answered it. "To the Institute for Dolphin Research. A team from Project Dolphin has been gathered there. You'll join it."

Pearson grimaced. The Institute was a horror house of memories for him, haunted by the ghosts of dolphins and his ex-wife. All along he had hoped that would not be part of it; all along he knew it would be. Slowly, he rose to go, but His Excellency had no intention of letting the meeting end on such an undramatic note.

"If that missile hadn't hit something as it came out of the tube, a massive nuclear strike would have been launched on friend and foe alike. This will not be the last attempt, gentlemen."

Hummscreech did not think so either.

CHAPTER EIGHT

Five hundred yards beyond the almost motionless herd, a shark slashed in the water, its rough skin like a rasp about to be drawn across velvet. Moody and dark on the outer edge of the circle, Longscreech turned his huge dark body in swift, sharp circles like a shark.

Within the circle, a thousand dolphins floated in the herd like chromosomes within a cell; each a single living trait, yet each a complete entity in itself. Longwhistle moved like the gene for grace; Longscreech moved like ferocity itself. Each dolphin moved, and was, one unique characteristic of the Self, which all combined to make. Each had its place in the totality, each had a position and a purpose in the total organism. Each individual was a distinct nuance of the Self as well.

Hummscreech floated at the middle of the herd, at the epicenter of understanding, counting the empty spaces the fifty had left; fifty irretrievably lost essences that would not return with next season's births or with any season's after. Hummscreech hung suspended between what-was and what-would-be.

His ranging echoes had slowed to the long, low-frequency hum for which he had been named and which indicated that he was in tune with the Flow of Things. His hum broke, climbed rapidly to an ultrasonic screech, and then stopped. His trance at an end, his mind shaped images for the rest.

The planet hung wet and fertile in the common mind, just as it hung in space. Beyond it, in the dark space between the stars, their enemy waited, malevolent yet impersonal as death. No longer cramped into the handful of shapes that had pursued them for so many eons through the dark water like a destiny, it waited to unleash its force.

Three hundred yards away, a shark sliced the water like a row of knives. Just outside the circle, Longscreech moved like a sinister desire, dark in the water like a palpable shadow.

Like a stomachless mouth, the other organism waited, lying off the planet like a body close to shore. As it had crouched just off a million other planets countless incarnations past, it crouched again, waiting for the Self to flee again, like a wolf waiting for a rabbit to break cover.

A hundred yards off, the shark blundered mindlessly along the dolphin spoor like a fool following a piece of string. Longscreech snapped his flukes and shot off at a tangent to the herd, like fangs going for the jugular.

In the common mind, the planet flared, pulsed with radiation, and erupted in flames at a thousand different points, just as they themselves bolted the planet like a startled hare. Then, over the image, like an alternative, the leprechaun face of a man burned into their awareness. Even before it became clear, Clickwhistle and Longwhistle began to move.

Just outside the circle, Longscreech turned on the shark and battered it to death.

CHAPTER NINE

Clickwhistle moved through the water like a muscle under skin, reading the distance, shape, and texture of the walls with low level clicks. Of all the cycles in his chain, of all the love-making, all the giving birth and being born, of all the times he had slid through death to come out on the other side a single conscious cell replicating itself, of all the circle of things behind him in that form, and of the few that still lay ahead, this was the moment he liked most.

His skin rippled with the stream of the water over his torpedo-shaped body, reducing the friction to zero. The echoes of his clicks came back hard and straight where the walls ran alongside him. They came back in herringbones where the walls joined to form the corners, and back in Vs where the rebounds from both corners met. He slid through his own echoes as easily as through the water. At a hundred yards, the walls were as tactile to him as if he had touched them, though their sound made no scratches in his velvet skin as the walls themselves would have done.

Halfway down the pool, he dipped his nose toward the bottom, curving his stomach and rounding his back so that his dorsal fin broke the surface like a knife. The air tickled it, and the water slid along it like a caress. At the interface of air and water, there was a mixture of sensations that delighted him almost as much as the echo of his ranging clicks bouncing back from behind the body of Longwhistle.

Were it not already fixed in a permanent smile, his dolphin mouth would have grinned even more. Everything was right; even the relative shortness of the pool did not bother him. The water was just right in the pool, warmed by the sun for half a morning; the warmth layered down toward the bottom in almost definable gradations to his ultrasensitive skin, and he could dive and feel it peel a degree at a time, level after level, like the transparent skin of an onion.

The texture of the water was smooth, and there was no chemical taste to it as there sometimes was. It was perfect water, and his whole body seemed to taste it as he flashed through it. Though the length of the pool kept him well below his top speed, he darted from end to end like a blue-gray streak. He had barely sent out his third set of ranging clicks when he passed through the echoes of the second. The rebound triangle had widened into a pyramid and the herringbone vibrations had flattened, rebounding more along his side than across his face.

The sound, while occupying only a small portion of his brain, still filled his life and the life of all dolphins with a kind of background music of a low key. The nuances of sound crisscrossed over him like the nuances of the water itself.

The whole interlocking ring of his existences moved with him as he moved through the water. As he moved through the present, the constant echoes of the past triangulated on him like the rebounds of his ranging clicks bouncing off the corners of the pool. He moved within a sheet of experience as contiguous as his skin.

He flattened a flipper on one side and smoothed the other, slipping himself into a half circle that glided him around in the other direction as his body followed his head in one smooth curve.

As his head went down, he clicked off the bottom just to catch the echoes along his stomach as he went by. Though he would not hear them in the way he heard his ranging clicks, his skin would still sense the subtle changes they made in the water. The air was like a feather drawn across the split fin of his flukes as they broke water on the last parabola of his turn.

They followed through and down behind him, moving him as rapidly in the opposite direction as if there had never been a turn. He rippled his body in a rapid undulation that increased his speed. He wanted a good start before he broke water completely, and the first two gyrations of his long body had already propelled him faster than he had been going before he had turned.

No sooner had he straightened in the new direction than he emitted a machine-gun burst of clicks toward the far end of the pool. There was no real need for them; the pool was already so familiar to him that he was certain of his position in relation to the walls without ranging. But he sent off his burst of sound to feel the echoes of her body, so much nicer and rounder and so much more complex than the rigid geometry of the pool.

He was snapping his tail for the second time, when the first of the echoes tingled along his lower jaw. The velvet of her skin gave off an echo as crinkly smooth as rumpled foil catching the light; it overrode and mixed with the narrow herringbone of the pool's shape with a delicious ambiguity. Between the clicks, he had sent out a higher frequency sound that came back to him with several levels of sensation.

The rough/smooth, soft/hard dichotomies of human perception were replaced by a hundred times more precise and more sensual feelings of texture and density, size and shape. From fifty yards away, Clickwhistle touched Longwhistle more intimately and completely than any human lover ever touched.

Where a human might see or feel only one surface at a time, Clickwhistle could hear *through* her, perceiving all sides of her at once. The echoes that went through her echoed off her again coming back, and Clickwhistle read her dorsal spine like a carom shot. Her flesh sounded like a halo around the distinct echo of the breast-shaped air sacs in her forehead. The sensation of her lingered like the red afterimage of a bright light through closed lids.

Still twenty yards away from her, he felt his second mixture of frequencies echo back from her as she wriggled in anticipation. He could taste her even at the far end of the pool, but the lubricant of her body spread on the water like a thick perfume as he neared her.

The taste was almost as subtle as the sound, and the two together interwove a pattern of textures and sensations that no human mind could begin to perceive. The interlocking pattern of taste and sound were the dolphin's color in the darkness of deep water, and the palette of Clickwhistle's senses had a variety of differences a thousand times greater than the nuances of color to a human eye.

From the clicks alone, he could draw the equivalent of more shades of blue than the eye of the most sensitive artist, and the taste of Longwhistle's body curved through more nuances in twenty yards than the finest graded spectrum human science or art could muster. In the second it took to cover the distance toward her, her taste had run through more shades of gold than any man could imagine. Each shade combined and interacted with the blues of her sound to form a kaleidoscope of patterns the permutations of which, on even one of the ten levels of Clickwhistle's awareness, would have overloaded the computer of *Dolphin Three*.

Complex though his mind was, it had to work feverishly with the permutations of Longwhistle's beauty. Every nuance of her constantly moving skin was connected directly to every nuance of her skin in the myriad incarnations of his past. The taste of her filled his mouth with a golden haze, and filtering the chemical messages of her desire triggered fountains of his own. His face split the invisible cloud of her desire like the prow of a ship as he sped toward her, and his own need outraced even his body as it flashed through the warm tropic water.

A few feet short of her, he flattened both flippers forward and snapped his flukes sharply downward, shooting himself up out of the water like a ten-foot arrow. He felt the rush of thin, dry air tingle his skin like the nap of velvet being brushed against the grain, and he anticipated the plunge back into the water that would brush the nap smooth again. He tingled, and the tingle flowed out of his mind and into hers as he reached the apex of his leap and bent himself downward.

Longwhistle arched herself in anticipation, and pressed her smooth white belly out as Clickwhistle's beak broke the surface of the water, which closed behind him with barely a ripple. His skin hummed like a sensitive antenna as it brushed along the length of her body. Her hard beak and smooth throat slid past his own and, in passing, started vibrations along the delicate midline of his underside.

His own lower lip stroked her undersurface like an exquisite blade that cleaves without cutting. In one swishing instant, the whole undersurfaces of their bodies slid past each other, their delicate skins contacting each other like ruffled velvet with a nerve in every hair.

Clickwhistle

Five times Clickwhistle darted away and curved back to leap, break water, and slide down her body like an elegant embrace that moves through time. They swam with increasing eddies of delight until the taste, sound, and texture had left them both almost dizzy.

Clickwhistle swooped across her body for the fifth time, pulling up like a "U" as his tail slipped across hers, and broke for the far end and one more dizzying dash, leap, slide. She let out a squeal that modulated into and out of the higher frequencies and undulated through thirty other frequencies like a wave.

Her love cry turned him around the pivot of his beak like a ball at the end of a string. With one swift downstroke of his tail, he propelled himself alongside her. Moving together as one body, they slid through the water the length of the pool and back.

They swam slowly, listening to their echoes stir up the bottom of time. The sonar of their minds overlapped the sonar of their ears and the sonar of their skins, and the pool clouded with delicious oils as they swam.

They thought of nothing except the overlapping and constantly changing patterns of their senses. Half of the levels of their minds played with the nuances of their pleasure in the present, matching and collating the texture and taste of the water, the new halftones of their ranging clicks since they had changed the chemistry of the water, the striations of warm and cool that laced the water, and the shower of sparks that was set off every time their skins rubbed smoothly over one another as they swam side by side in the pool.

Halfway back along the pool, the chill of Dr. Rathgall's presence on the island fell across Longwhistle's consciousness like a shadow, and she shivered.

43

CHAPTER TEN

Pearson stood along the edge of the pool staring toward the seaward end. He watched the waves slap against the rocks, break over them, and run down into the pool. Behind him, under the balcony, the water ran out again down a concrete sluice and back into the ocean on the far side of the point of rock on which the Institute for Dolphin Research had been built. For a second, he could see the blood on the rocks. He turned away hurriedly and walked back under the terrace and up the circular metal stairs to the balcony.

The metal steps clanged under his feet as they had the day Sonny had gone up on the rocks. The place suddenly exploded with echoes, and the high-pitched distress call of the dying dolphin cut the warm Caribbean air like a silken noose. He paused halfway up the stairs, his head pounding. It had been a week since he had been plunged physically into his past like that and it unnerved him.

He took the last turn and a half a step at a time, but his head emerged above the deck of the balcony still flushed. A balding man he did not recognize rose to greet him, the other man remained seated. It was Rathgall, a whale of a man with tiny black eyes and a penchant for white shirts even in the tropics.

There was no need for introductions; the men had been enemies for years. Every theory Pearson had advanced Rathgall had attacked. The fat man had made

44

a career of dogging Pearson's progress and snapping at
its loose ends. If there were four hundred pages of valid
data, and one paragraph of conjecture, Rathgall would
seize upon the latter and build an experiment and a
rebuttal around it.

Pearson was not a meticulous scholar; though his
thinking was rigorous, he had too much imagination for
the academic community, to which Rathgall directed the
articles which made him a favorite among the anthro-
pocentric, who ran scared at Pearson's hint that the
dolphin was perhaps more intelligent than man. He was
no favorite of Pearson's; Rathgall's niggling had cost him
two grants and had almost shut down one of his early
projects.

Pearson stopped on the top step and glared at Rathgall.
For an instant, the man's face disappeared in a mass of
sharks, tearing at the man, the walls, and each other in
indiscriminate frenzy.

"Dr. Pearson," the balding man said, "I'm Dr. Fallow
and this, as you may know, is Dr. Rathgall."

Rathgall nodded and smiled his killer whale smile.

"What the hell is he doing here?" Pearson snapped.

"I'm here to keep you on your toes as usual, dear boy.
Kirby's orders, you know."

Pearson turned to the other doctor. "Get him out of
here."

"I'm sorry, Dr. Pearson, but I have no authority over
Dr. Rathgall. In fact, he's my superior."

"And yours, Pearson, as head of this project."

Pearson ignored him and addressed Fallow. "Look, I
didn't ask for this job. I can't work with him here. I've
seen him around dolphins before. If he gets within fifty
feet of them, they go into a panic and it takes days to get
them calmed down again."

Rathgall raised a finger of protest. "Ahh, dear boy, I won't be in your lab. I'm only here to see to it that your reports are cleared of fantasy before we pass them on. You have such a tendency to make the intuitive leap that so damages your data, you know."

Pearson looked at him fiercely and then turned away. Something in Rathgall called out a hatred in him beyond all reason, a blind fury that always puzzled him. He squeezed the rail of the balcony and looked down into the crystal water of the outer pool.

It was filled with blood and the flashing fins of sharks, and one arm floating free for a minute in a white shirt sleeve. He blinked and it was gone. The vision was something new, and it frightened him. He had almost gotten used to being plunged into his past without warning, but this hallucination was an aberration of a different magnitude. He was pale as he turned back toward the other men.

"You don't look very well, Doctor. Did you swallow something that upset you?" Rathgall's reference to the drug he had once taken enraged him again, and he turned back to the rail and looked down hoping to see Rathgall among the sharks again. Instead, there was only clear water. He spoke over his shoulder to Dr. Fallow. "Where are the dolphins?"

"In the inner pool; they were outside until Dr. Rathgall came; then they went inside."

"Yes, well, they won't be back out until you get this fat jackal off the island."

Rathgall laughed. "No need to worry, Doctor. I'll be down the coast most of the time, just coming over here every few days to see how you're doing. I have my own setup at Point St. George. Somewhat different than yours, I imagine."

Pearson snorted. "Don't tell me His Excellency's Council on Science is letting you practice on animals again."

Rathgall stiffened; his tiny black eyes flashed anger. "If you will remember, Doctor, I won that case in the Court of Major Appeals."

"Well, you'll find out operant conditioning won't work on these subjects, Doctor—with or without your electric thumbscrews."

Rathgall laughed patronizingly. "Ahh, Pearson, what a scientist you'd be if it weren't for your flamboyant sense of the dramatic. But then I understand it puts you in good stead now that you've joined the mystics."

Pearson looked up at the clouds scudding by over the lip of the island to the southeast. "There's more to science than statistics, Rathgall."

"Perhaps." There was ice in Rathgall's voice. "But His Excellency is looking for scientific answers, not daydreams, and you can be sure I won't pass on to him any of your mystic intuitions without hard evidence to back them up." Pearson studied the clouds, and Rathgall raised his voice. "Let me remind you of one thing, Doctor; if you claim a result, you had better be able to reproduce it. There'll be no more talking dolphins only you can understand."

Pearson squeezed the railing and looked out across the pool. A fin flashed toward the far end. He blinked his eyes to clear them, but it was still there, traveling like a rocket toward the rocks. He tried to look away, but he could not. Just where he knew it would, just short of the rocks, the dolphin's beak broke water like the nose of a missile.

The long, shiny body followed the beak like the hull of a missile launched from a submarine. It sailed up like a missile triggering a global defense system. Up and onto the rocks, crashing onto the jagged points, scraping over their ridges; being spun around as one dug deep into its side and hooked it, whirling it around and slamming its head sidewards against another rock.

The newspaper lay where he had just thrown it, shouting down to Cathy in the pool, "The bastards! They've turned it into a weapon!"

His shrill cries like a tiny siren, Sonny twitched to free himself from the boulder that had pierced him like a lance. In the pool below, Cathy screamed and screamed. He ran down the circular metal stairs while the rising/ falling distress call stung the air like a wire. He ran along the pool and scrambled up onto the rocks beside the dying dolphin. He cradled its head in his lap, looking into that eye that looked back at him with something between pity and exasperation.

He waved Cathy back down off the rocks, the blood soaking into his terry-cloth pool jacket. The sun reflected off the slick skin, on which the gashes showed up dull, like erasures on a photograph. He heard the high-pitched Donald Duck voice, which came so close time after time to mimicking what they had said in the lab, say almost as clear as his own voice, "into a weapon," and die, with what Pearson still heard as a sigh of disgust.

He was sweating and shaking when he opened his eyes. The rocks were bare. It was another "residual" from the drug he had taken almost five years before. The pool below him was empty also. He was cold despite the tropic weather, and his teeth chattered like a dolphin clacking its discontent.

Dr. Fallow was next to him now. "Are you all right, Doctor?"

Pearson nodded uncertainly. Rathgall had come up on the other side of him. "Another hallucination, Doctor?" There was a mock solicitousness in the voice that made Pearson want to grab Rathgall and fling him over the balcony.

"Fuck you, Rathgall."

The fat man laughed. "Well, enough pleasantries for one day. You'll find sonic equipment in the lab. I'll be working on electrical stimulation and carrying on a few experiments with the natural enemies of these creatures, just to make sure the presence of enough sharks wouldn't drive them into that kind of panic. I'll be back in a few days to see how you're doing with your series." He turned and waddled away toward the terrace doors and the inside stairs.

Dr. Fallow helped Pearson to a chair near the small, glass-topped table and poured him a drink. Pearson pushed it away and shook his head. He concentrated instead on his respirations, slowing them, concentrating on them until his mind emptied and he relaxed. He sat with his eyes closed for several minutes before he spoke to the other doctor.

"How many dolphins?" he said finally.

"Only two. We had five coming down from the Marine Institute, but the plane crashed."

Pearson stood up. "Let's take a look."

The men went in through the terrace door and down the inside stairs into the lab. It was quiet in the pool until he got within twenty feet of the steel door that separated the lab from the pool area, and then the whistling, low, began, low and rhythmic and accompanied by clicks and ranging signals.

When he opened the door, he was greeted with a symphony of whistles and clacking, clapping of flippers and barks and clicks that crescendoed as he approached the pool. Pearson smiled. Certainly he had never seen them before, and yet they were familiar to him.

Dr. Fallow introduced him to a third man, a young dark-haired man who carried a clipboard and wore a white lab coat and looked like every graduate lab assistant Pearson had ever seen. "This is Dr. Robert Baker, Dr. Pearson. He's worked with dolphins with the Hydrodynamic Center at Port Hernandez."

Baker extended his hand and smiled. "I worked with Kramer on the synthetic skin for the Dolphin System," he said. "We took a lot from your early work, but then I guess everyone connected with the Project would have to say that. How you managed to know that the laminar flow occurred because of a reduced Reynold's number just from an autopsy, I'll never know. But it certainly put us on the right track." Pearson smiled; the theory had gotten him everything from scorn to a seat on His Excellency's Council on Science.

Baker went on. "And your account of the wrinkling of the underbelly in their turns allowed us to make the quantum jump in the synthetic skin." His voice was full of admiration. "Thanks to you, the speed of *Dolphin Four* is just about limitless once we get a better sonar. Without it, *Dolphin Four* would be puttering along at forty knots like the rest of the fleet."

Pearson looked puzzled until he realized how few people would know about *Dolphin Four* until His Excellency decided to release news of it. Probably he and Rathgall were the only ones on the island who knew.

He turned to the pool. "Both *tursiops*," he noted.

"Yes," Baker said. "Caught just off the island too. I understand the male there practically swam into the net. The female swam along trying to free him, then she jumped in too. Good thing, too, or we wouldn't have any specimens. Five were supposed to be flown down from the Marine Institute but the plane crashed on take-off; whole electrical system suddenly failed on them."

Pearson nodded noncommittally. Baker held out his clipboard. "Would you like to see the lab inventory? The ultra sound rig will shatter glass." Pearson looked at him as if he were mad. Baker shrugged. "You'll need it for the series of tests Dr. Rathgall left for you to carry out in the next three days."

The young man lowered his eyes. "It's not for me to say really, but I think it's kind of arrogant for him to leave a series of tests like that as if he were still project head or something."

Pearson snorted. "He *is.*"

The young man's mouth formed a small "O" and he frowned. "I thought . . . that is, I was told I'd be working with you, Dr. Pearson, and I assumed that once you got here you'd . . . I mean especially since you were proved right so many times when Dr. Rathgall wrote all those papers against your theories. I mean . . ."

Fallow tried to change the subject. "Will you be beginning the tests immediately, Doctor?"

Baker interrupted. "I don't want to cause any dissension on the project, sir, but to make someone of your stature subordinate to Dr. Rathgall, I mean, it's preposterous."

Fallow glared at the young man, and Pearson smiled his leprechaun smile. "Doctor, my reputation has slipped somewhat since I left the field. You did hear about my breakdown, I presume."

"Certainly, sir, but that drug was found to have the same effect on anyone, no matter how stable. Why, even the drug subculture avoided it! Besides, it's not relevant to your work in dolphin research. You're practically the father of delphinology."

Pearson frowned ruefully. "No," he said, "all I did was rediscover what Hebb, Lilly, and Essapian found and then had suppressed after the fighting. We'd all be years ahead if we had access to their works.

Baker frowned. "With all due respect, sir, they were Americans, sir, nationalists of the worst order. I mean men like that, however brilliant, had to be suppressed. Why, we'd have no hemispheric government if we let those old nationalists surface again."

Pearson nodded absently. It was a familiar cant and one he had long since stopped trying to refute. He shrugged. "Still, it would have saved a lot of lives."

"Lives?"

"Dolphin lives, Dr. Baker. Christ, if I could have seen Morgane and McFarland's work on anesthesia when I first started, I wouldn't have killed four dolphins."

A dolphin lay in front of him on a hospital roll cart. Dr. Harris was giving it a shot of Nembutal one tenth as strong as anything they had used on other animals. In less than a minute, it began to slip into a coma and its breathing began to disintegrate. The others stood there just staring at one another in disbelief. A human infant would have been able to tolerate the dose they had given the dolphin.

In five minutes it was dead. It would be the same the next day when they tried another drug, and it would not be until the fourth one that they would realize that dolphin breathing was voluntary and that a loss of consciousness meant death. One after another he watched them smother, their breathing getting more and more erratic until it fell apart completely, until the fourth looked at him with that odd mixture of pity and reproach.

"Are you all right, Doctor?" Baker was staring at him. He was sweating again, and he was cold at the same time. He closed his eyes and focused on his breathing. In thirty seconds, it was back to normal. He smiled at Baker. "A little leftover from the experiment. It comes and goes."

Fallow understood. Pearson's mental lapses and behavior had become legendary. Since his breakdown, almost everyone in two fields had some anecdote about him. Pearson wondered if that would be coming back too. He remembered so little of it, except living in a very foggy place full of teeth and dissections. He pulled his mind away from it before it triggered another "residual."

"Will you want to start the experiments right away, Doctor?" Fallow asked.

Pearson shook his head. He had had only an hour's sleep since the men had come for him. Perhaps it was that triggering all of the "residuals." Perhaps a few hours' rest would clear his head. He wondered how much sleep he could afford. There was probably less than a day before *Dolphin Three* would be on station with its new coating of Kramer's synthetic.

He would know for sure when it had become a target when His Excellency made the report on *Dolphin Four* public. He wondered what His Excellency was telling the Non-SEAPACT nations about the explosion that must have rocked the ocean floor off the Mid-Atlantic rise. Whatever it was, they would not be buying it. There wasn't much time for sleep, and yet there was no way he could go without it.

"No," he said to Fallow, "I think I'll get some sleep first." He smiled ruefully. "I wouldn't want to hallucinate any results."

He walked closer to the pool. The male was half out

of the water, whistling and barking as he approached. Pearson knelt alongside the pool and looked. The dolphin scooted toward him on his tail, almost laughing as he did. It was the same trick Sonny used to greet him with whenever he came close enough to the pool.

But this dolphin looked nothing like Sonny; he was too big, too mottled along the sides, and yet there was a distinct quality to the voice that reminded him of the dolphin he had raised for seven years, the dolphin his wife had lived with in the half-flooded lab for six months, the dolphin that had performed hundreds of experiments, had spoken perhaps a thousand words with some perfection, and then had thrown himself onto the rocks.

He grabbed a mullet from the bucket near the edge of the pool and threw it over the dolphin's head. The dolphin scooted backwards on his tail and caught it with a sharp clack of his jaws and disappeared under water. Pearson smiled at his own foolishness. Sonny would have thrown it back the first time.

He was about to go when the water in front of him erupted around a streamlined form that shot up out of it, curved at the top of his leap, and with a sidewards flick, tossed the fish back at him just before he broke the surface of the water in his downward plunge.

The dolphin's head appeared above the water near the side of the pool, making the series of clicks and whistles that approximate human laughter. Under its raucous guffawing a murmur of other sound ran, audible enough to be noticed but not loud enough to be decipherable. Pearson leaned closer and strained his ears until he heard the words, ". . . onny goo . . . boie."

Pearson thrust himself back from the pool, knocking over the bait bucket. The dolphin turned toward him and fixed him with its gleaming eye. Then, it seemed to give a wink and a final laugh and disappeared back under the water. Baker and Fallow helped him to his feet.

"That kind of vocalization's odd in an untrained animal," Fallow said.

Baker clucked over him like a hen over a lost chick. "Do you need any help getting upstairs, Doctor?"

Pearson shook his head. He could not keep his hands still, and by the time he got to the door, he understood that they were shaking from fear. What had unnerved him was not the sound of his dead dolphin's voice repeating the first phrase he had taught it. What had terrified him, what had sent him sprawling in panic back over the bait bucket, was the picture of a killer whale, suspended in the foggy water over the curving deck of a submarine, a whale at which dolphin after dolphin hurled himself in suicidal assault.

CHAPTER ELEVEN

Pearson wakened to the gentle nudging of Baker. He awoke slowly, blinking himself toward an illusive consciousness. The electric light hurt his eyes and seemed to drive him back into oblivion. It was like trying to waken from anesthesia.

"Dr. Pearson." There was an oddly husky tone to Baker's voice. "I'm sorry to wake you, but I thought you'd want to know."

For a terrible instant, the young man looked so much like the graduate assistant who had worked with him on the first dolphin experiments that he expected to be told that another of the three dolphins had starved himself to death. The young man hesitated, and Pearson waited for the ax to fall.

"The *Dolphin*'s gone." He spoke as if telling Pearson that a mutual loved one had perished during the night, and looked as if he expected some words of consolation from the older scientist. Pearson could only stare at him blankly. For an instant he almost said, "Turn them loose! Turn them all loose! I'm closing the Institute."

Baker leaned forward and said it again, and Pearson groaned. The thought of another series of suicides tormented him more than he could admit even to himself. He thought of the big male dolphin, the remarkable mottled one whose like he had never seen before, and of the graceful female as well. Certainly all dolphins were graceful, but that one was something special, as Sonny had been something special.

All dolphins he had ever seen seemed to have some unique characteristic that set them apart. None of them were ever ciphers, and the death of all of them had hurt, even in the beginning when they had been just another laboratory animal to him. When the first one had stopped breathing, it had been as if he had lost a real patient. He had stared at it in disbelief, as if in another moment, someone would come along and it would not have happened at all.

"Which one?" he asked.

"Four," Baker answered. It seemed an effort for the man to get the words out. Pearson looked at him blankly, trying to understand why if the dolphins were no more to the young man than numbers, their death could have struck him so forcefully. It was a puzzle he was still too much asleep to comprehend.

"The male or the female?" he asked finally.

"Male or female, sir?" Baker wondered if there were some special code that designated one submarine from another, perhaps the Pacific ones were female and the Atlantic ones male, or vice versa. Either way, the code was beyond him, and he could do nothing but ask again. "Male or female?"

Pearson blinked his eyes and shook his head as if trying to rouse himself from a trance. "I'm sorry," he said, "I must still be half asleep. Which of the dolphins is dead?"

"*Dolphin Four*. His Excellency just announced it. Its power plant apparently blew up just this side of the Mid-Atlantic Rise."

Pearson nodded solemnly. *Dolphin Three* was ready; the clock was running again. Baker seemed to be waiting for some kind of comfort. Pearson had none to offer.

The best he could do was mumble, "I thought you were talking about the two dolphins down in the pool," before he lay back groggily and closed his eyes. He was asleep again before Baker left the room.

CHAPTER TWELVE

When Pearson awoke again, the light Baker had left on was still burning. His eyes were open, but he seemed no more able to rise than if he were asleep. He lay on his back staring up at the ceiling. It was off-white; like the walls, a plastic surface, flawless and smooth as a dolphin's skin.

He was sure he was awake, and yet he felt water rushing by his body, and his skin rippling to accommodate it. He shook his head, and his body seemed to veer in the water. He shook it again, and the feeling stopped. As he looked around the room, he had the unshakable feeling that either he or the room had just stopped moving.

It had been an instant of complete dissociation. He had not been himself for an instant. He had been—he did not know what—but he *did* know that whatever it was, it had not been him.

He tried to deal with it rationally, tried to include it as a new symptom in a familiar syndrome. The sudden flights into the past were "residuals" of the drug, triggered perhaps by stress and the old surroundings again, perhaps even by a lack of sleep. The vision of Rathgall being mutilated by the sharks was a blurring of reality more serious than simply a replayed memory. But the last feeling was something of a different magnitude entirely, a truly psychotic symptom. Complete dissociation of the self meant schizophrenia. He wondered for a moment if that had been what he had been waiting for all along. Ever since the drug, he had been waiting for something to happen; perhaps this was it, the final disintegration of his sanity.

Pearson smiled to himself and shook his head. It would be nothing that trivial, and he recognized the diagnosis as another attempt to evade what was about to happen. Under the drug, he had known exactly what it was, but when he came out of it, he seemed to have forgotten it. Yet it seemed always on the tip of his tongue, as if he were constantly about to tell himself what it was.

He wondered if his breakdown had not been just a way of silencing that tongue, until the knowledge could be forced into hiding at a deeper level. Under the drug he had known what the breakdown had allowed him to forget until it had receded into only the vague certainty that something was coming.

He was sitting in Burroughs' living room, thoroughly aware of everything around him, yet completely blind. He could hear them talking all around him. Burroughs' calm, measured speech overrode the other chipmunk voices with an almost catchy note of panic in them. Someone was saying, "My god, he's overdosed; you've got to get him to a hospital!"

He thought it was Burroughs' wife. He could hear Burroughs saying, "It's all right, John. It's only temporary. It will pass in a few minutes, just don't panic." He couldn't really hear the words, but he could hear the tone, and the steadiness that told him everything was under control. He waited like a pilot for landing instructions.

He wasn't really afraid. There was only one way to gather subjective data and that was by direct experience. No mouse could report on the psychic effect of the drug.

Certainly, it was that argument that had made him agree to be Burroughs' guinea pig. And then too, Burroughs had assured him that while it might be bizarre, it would not be dangerous or even lasting.

Of course, he knew that Burroughs was only hoping that what he said was true. Still, if it was dangerous, only a scientist as disciplined as Pearson could be expected to keep control of himself long enough to describe what was happening to him. And he had been doing just that at first.

Just sitting there in Burroughs' living room, talking out loud to no one in particular, knowing the tape recorder would pick everything up. Concentrating on the symptoms and trying to get precisely the right word for each sensation. Using as much of his biochemistry as he could to explain what he thought was happening, looking for telltale physiological signs.

Marking the respiratory changes in vision that left everything kind of watery. And the changes in his other senses as well, an increased tactility to all of his skin, a vastly increased sense of hearing as if—how had he said it?—as if he were hearing-himself-hearing-himself-hearing.

He could feel Burroughs monitoring him with the electrodes and reading off measurements, and he thought how incongruous it was to be so wired up like that in a private living room at what seemed to be more a party than an experiment.

He was very coherent for the first hour or so, and everything was perfectly clear to him, though afterwards it would be just a jumble of images which would fade out of his mind like a volatile gas. And then everything changed.

"There's someone inside my body!" he said. The others laughed because he seemed so amazed at what he had discovered, but they of course did not understand what he meant.

"Of course, John! *You* are," Burroughs said good-naturedly.

"No, someone *else*, some*thing* else. No, force isn't right; being, that's it. A being!"

Burroughs was talking, but the sounds seemed to come at him from all corners of the room. He could hear the echoes of Burroughs' words at the same time he could hear the words themselves, as if Burroughs were speaking to him in an auditorium and he was close enough to hear both the speaker's words and the half-second delay over the loudspeakers, just a little out of phase. And it felt so good that he wanted Burroughs to go on talking forever.

Later, he told himself that he had listened to Burroughs' voice because it soothed him, but even then he knew it wasn't true. He was not listening to the voice at all but using it to feel everything in the room. He could actually feel the shapes of everyone in the room. For the first time in his life he had the feeling of actually being in space, actually occupying a specific kind of relationship with the room around him.

He could actually feel where he was in relation to everything in the room, actually feel the relationship between all sides of everything in the room and himself. It was like suddenly being able to see in three-dimensional color after so long seeing in two-dimensional black and white.

He had stopped talking into the tape. He was hearing everything with such clarity and with so many dimensions that he had no idea how long he had forgotten to talk. He opened his mouth to say something and his own echo came ringing back, even more sharply delineating the room and everything in it. But he couldn't hear what he was saying because the content of his sound had become not the contents of his mind but the contents of the room.

What he was hearing was not sound but the room itself, and everyone in it. It seemed bizarre to him to be hearing people instead of seeing them, and yet it was, and that part was what scared him later whenever he thought of it, it was familiar also, like something he had done a long, long time before and had forgotten about. He made some more sounds and listened to them come back, overlapping Burroughs' sounds and his own previous sounds.

There was something almost lascivious about the way the women sounded, the way they rounded the sounds and softened them, although Burroughs with his fatness did it almost as well as they did. He could not get over how they felt and that he was feeling/hearing them holographically, from all sides at once, like whole, three-dimensional beings. Even when he thought about what a poor thing sight was to let him perceive only the side of an object that was facing him, he did not realize that he had gone blind. Nor did he mind it when he did realize it.

He had an impulse to get up and walk through the sounds as they came pinging back off the walls and the bookcase and the furniture. He had an impulse to turn and talk in one direction after another to see how people felt when the sound came from different directions and bounced off them.

CHAPTER THIRTEEN

And then he began to hear the echoes on his skin, like thin waves rippling onto the beach of a bay, and he forgot about hearing for a minute and just felt. He had always had a habit of touching things, of picking them up and fondling them, of getting to know things so much more concretely by handling them. Never, for instance, knowing his anatomy until he had actually taken an organism apart and held the tissue in his hands and felt the relationships between what had been removed and what still remained.

But this was different; he could feel his own skin touching things. Not the way it usually is, not something touching his skin, something pressing, however gently, against him. Now he could feel the skin itself feeling things, could feel how it gave way before things and then surged back along them on the outside taking their imprint and passing it on. Measuring texture and depth and weight all at once, but with more accuracy than ever before.

He thought of how great a surgeon would be with that sensation, and he made a mental note to tell Burroughs about it. And then he thought of lovers and made a note to tell Burroughs about that application as well, except that, just then, Mrs. Burroughs put her hand on his bare arm because something was wrong, and he realized that almost no one could take the intensity of love-making in that state, so excruciatingly pleasant did the touch of a hand feel. He could feel the whorl of her finger tips, and his own skin retreating from and then surging back to fill in the tiny crevices that marked it, whorl after whorl.

He became suddenly aware of the intimate relationship between the space in which things happened and the event itself. He began to feel the room, not merely hear it as a physical thing, but to actually feel the space between himself and the walls pressing on his skin. He could feel the distance between him and the bookcase and between himself and Burroughs. It did not dawn on him for what seemed like hours that what he was feeling was the air in the room.

He could feel how it pressed down on every part of him, and of how it disturbed in patterns like the sound when people moved in it. It was like suddenly being aware that you are frozen in a kind of malleable plastic, and that space between object and object was not empty at all but was full—full of air, a real physical presence of which he had lost awareness.

He wondered how to tell Burroughs that the air was a matrix that made every experiment a different one; that any movement made the room a different room; that nothing was ever still or the same. Air was present and he could feel it; it had infinitely more nuances than vision and almost as many as sound.

The ability to feel the air elated him, but his elation was followed immediately like a shadow by a familiar feeling that frightened him. The air felt different than it had ever felt before, yet that very difference was familiar. He tried to rationalize that the familiarity of it was simply that that was how he had felt the air when he had been an infant and had had no restraints on his senses, had not been trained to use some and repress others, that it was the way things had felt before his infant eyes had focused and he had begun to become a visual organism.

But the frightening thing was that he knew that the memory came from much longer ago than that, and what was worse, he felt the strangeness of the air in relation to the way he had felt another medium, a medium much more pervasive, much more filled with tactile data than air. At first, he thought of water and then he felt it as some liquid even more viscous than that.

A medium capable of carrying all the nuances he was capable of receiving, and he realized what a poor medium water was and what an even poorer medium air was. But the memory of that other medium was so old, so very old, that it terrified him even more than the intimate memory of how things felt in water and of the quantum differences between feeling in water and in air. And then he realized that what he remembered was not how air felt, but how *different* air felt from water.

He began to panic again because there was some reason why he knew sensations he could not ever have experienced, and he was afraid to know what that reason was. And beyond that, there was another set of memories that were more frightening still because they denied all the premises on which his sanity was based. The ancient memories from which he withheld himself were at once inescapable and yet unthinkable.

It unnerved him that he kept thinking what a poor medium air was if you stayed in it for very long because you couldn't taste anything in it. But the taste of the air distracted him from that frightening train of thought, and he began to taste the room as well as hear and feel it. For a minute, he tried to tell himself that he was experiencing simply an increased sense of smell, and that he was mistranslating it as a sense of taste, forgetting that most of taste was really determined by smell anyway.

But he could not pull it over on himself. He was tasting the room, not smelling it. He could taste Burroughs' aftershave lotion, and the acrid cleaner's acid on someone's tweed vest. He could actually taste the people, his friends and Burroughs' friends, wives and husbands, and it almost made him laugh that he knew everyone in the room more intimately than anyone else had ever known them, had tasted them in a way that even a lover could not taste them, had heard them in a way no one could even feel them, and felt them in a way no one could even see them.

He could taste every function of their bodies and the relationship of them to the room, and the taste of the tape as it ran across the metallic tape heads. He was intimate with the room and everything in it on a variety of levels the rest could not even guess at. For a second it embarrassed him, but it did not repulse him, that two of them had made love before coming to the gathering.

Even though his sensing of the people around him had ceased to be scientific and had become purely hedonistic, he knew it to be valuable, even if none of it were transcribed. He realized that he could never hate any of those people after knowing them so intimately, and he wondered if perhaps that wasn't the most important discovery he would make.

He began, out of the welter of sensation, to pick an overriding taste, one that was familiar and yet unfamiliar, obvious yet beyond his grasp. He chuckled as he realized it was the taste of himself, the taste that spread out from his body on the air so much less acutely than in the water and yet strongly enough for him to perceive. He began to understand the intuitive things that were said about the "flavor" of a party or a place.

The plain had been complex, where there had been only a surface, there were now surfaces under surfaces, and he was sure he had not touched bottom yet. There was another dimension that he was missing, though he could feel the first dimensions increasing in complexity as he began to be aware of the nuances of sound and feeling and taste expanding in combination into an almost infinite variety of permutations. And then he realized what it was that made the variety infinite—it was Time.

The new dimension popped into his head like lights coming on in a room where there had been only the dimmest of candlelight. It brought everything into sharper focus and yet blurred each thing together with not only every other thing but with itself. Each sensation became the first in an infinite progression like a real hand held between opposing mirrors. Time replicated sensation out to an infinity on all sides.

He looked at a sensation like a real hand and then let his awareness drift up the sensation to the limitless line of hands that extended from it through time. He ran his awareness up the repetitive chain of timed events until he slipped into the final step.

Just as the final step is not being able to distinguish the real hand from the reflection, Pearson let himself slip into time and discover another truth. His sensations ran not only backward into the immediate past, they ran back into past after past. They ran back, and this frightened him, life cycle after life cycle, incarnation after incarnation, and each and all of them affected and were integral with every present experience. The present on all levels was contiguous with everything in the past.

But there was something beyond even that, because

way back behind all the sequences of John Pearson there was another sequence of cycles, an alien series of cycles whose pure foreignness made him cringe. But more terrifying was that behind that alien cycle was a cycle more alien and foreign still, something he could not yet entertain even as a possibility. It was too much to know, and even thinking about it risked being inadvertently drawn into it.

He followed the ramifications of things backward through time and arrived at an understanding that so terrified him, was so much beyond his ability to comprehend, that it had unbalanced him completely for almost a year. Not until he had safely hidden all traces of his discovery from himself by selectively forgetting it and repressing it was he able to come back out into the world.

And that unbearable truth was what was coming, the truth he had been dreading and waiting for so long, and he knew it was what he had been brought back to the Institute to find again.

After a year, he had been able to go back to Burroughs and ask to hear the tape, knowing that it might tell him the truth he could not bear to know. The last part of the tape almost sent him back to the institution again.

The first part was strictly scientific, but what was scientific became poetic, and then incoherent, and finally silent. But what terrified him, what had made him shun his whole field of delphinology, was that the last third of the tape, the part where he had thought he was babbling out the amazing and mind-boggling understandings he was coming to, was nothing more than half an hour of clicks and high-pitched whistles, and, near the end, the rising/falling whistle of a dolphin in distress.

CHAPTER FOURTEEN

Pearson found himself sitting on the edge of the bed, shaking. For a moment, he was sure where he was, and then he was not.

Cathy turned to him and said, "He was human, you know. He was better than human. You remember how he got me over my fear of his teeth?"

He nodded. He remembered how Sonny had conditioned her, how he had held a ball in his jaws so that he couldn't bite down and then had run his mouth up and down her legs. He remembered how, day by day, the dolphin had rolled the ball back in his mouth until there was nothing to stop the teeth from closing except his will and the fact that she had gotten used to it, even liked the teeth moving over her like a caress.

"What human would have had the patience to do that?" she asked.

Pearson nodded. It was like a eulogy. What could be said against the dead. And besides, he had felt it too, something far different than the relationship between master and pet. Something very much like friendship, like an equal affection between members of a different species. He wondered if it was not possible to love something that was not human.

"There were things that weren't in the report," she said. "Things I felt about him. I would have felt foolish writing them down. He understood, you know. He *knew*."

Pearson nodded; what else could he do but agree? It was true, Sonny was something different, even he had felt it.

"I loved him like a little brother," she said.

"I know," he said. He did not say that he had come down late one night unexpectedly and had seen her swimming nude with the dolphin, side by side with him, free and innocent as children. She rarely wore the tank top anyway except when somebody came down to look in on the experiment, and without it she looked like a mermaid. He could still see her, her slim fingers over the dolphin's fin, her arm around his back like children walking across a playground.

"You don't care?" she said.

Oddly perhaps, he didn't. There was no way he could be jealous of it. He assumed it was possible to love two people in different ways, and he had almost gotten used to thinking of Sonny as people. He didn't think it rational to demand all of someone's affection, and he was surprised that she had apparently expected him to demand all of hers.

For him, it was enough that they got along well, worked well together, still communicated. For him, it was a marriage built on mutual admiration and a common consuming interest, and nothing could damage that.

"Could you have felt any different if I had?" he asked.

She shook her head and he shrugged. In a week she would be gone without even saying good-by. When he finally went to look for her, she would elude him. "Then what would it matter?" he said. "People do what they have to do."

He did not mention that he had seen her from the balcony the night before Sonny went up on the rocks, swimming naked as usual alongside the dolphin. She did not tell him of her premonition or that she had been saying good-by, that she had been crying. She did not even tell him that she had seen him on the balcony.

She said, "I just wanted to get it out, you understand. I don't know, I could never put it in the reports, and I always felt I'd cheated him in some way."

Pearson nodded; somehow he understood.

"The night before he killed himself . . ." she said. He nodded. They had always communicated a lot in silences; it had been a comfortable relationship, a friendship almost.

"I knew . . ." she said.

For an instant he could feel the water along his dorsal fin and feel her breasts bobbing against him in the water, could feel the roughness of her arm as it slid over him as he swam. He could taste the odd flavor of her tears in the water and could hear the curious droning human voice mumbling something about the rocks he could almost understand.

He looked up at the ceiling. The room seemed to have been moving again, and he seemed to be slipping.

CHAPTER FIFTEEN

Pearson waited for the room to move again. It didn't. He was shivering and sweating at the same time. He got up slowly. He had an impulse to go downstairs, but he could not quite remember for what. He was hungry and there would be food down in the refrigerator in the lab, a Coke at least, perhaps even some cold cuts. At any rate it would stop him from dreaming; if he was lucky it might even stop him from thinking.

In the lab he fumbled for the light switch, then crossed the room to the refrigerator and opened it. A few bottles of Coke, no food. "Foolish to have expected it," he thought. He took a Coke and pushed the door behind as he turned.

In the middle of the floor was a large Plexiglas case without a top. A drain at one end gave it a flow-through current. He remembered when he had built it, a long time before. It kept the dolphins' weight from pressing on their lungs and suffocating them when they were operated on, but it didn't save them from the thin straw-like pipes he drove into their brains as sleeves for the electrodes. Still, he had administered a local anesthetic, and he was sure the pain was negligible.

Every time he drove one, he thought of it, of being the captive of some alien species and having the same thin metal sleeves driven into his own skull for the same purpose. He always thought of curious aliens making thrust

73

after thrust down the sleeve with electrodes, feeling for the different centers of the brain until they hit the pleasure center and he groaned out some sort of unthinking response.

Suddenly he was in the tank, lying on his side, one eye out of the water and one in, watching the men moving around him, aware of what they were about to do to him, yet harboring no malice toward them. They were what they were, and there was no holding them responsible for that. And besides, he had agreed to it.

He felt the narrow circle of pipe edge pressing on the delicate outer surface of his skin. The man was resting it lightly, twirling it ever so slightly between his finger and thumb before he hit it with the hammer. The end was sharp, and though it did not break the skin, it gave an eerie cutting feeling, as if a small circle of skin were being excised.

And then it plunged, driven deep by the hammer, and a laser beacon of pain shot out of him toward Clickwhistle's brain and through it to the rest of the Self waiting a few miles offshore. The spear of pain made them all wince, though none of them would have given up their part of the pain and returned it to the dolphin that twitched only slightly under its impact because he was being relieved of the greater part of his pain by the common mind.

The eye out of the water blinked, and the glow receded in it for a moment. The eye in the water stared down at the floor through the Plexiglas bottom of the case. It too blinked as the second thin spear of metal shot through the flesh and into the brain. He shivered in the tank as the others winced in the sea, and flicked water out of the tank with his flukes, over the side of the case and dripping down onto the hammer.

Clickwhistle

The wet head of the hammer slipped off the top of the electrode as it hit. The sleeve went only halfway in and had to be hit a second time. The second hit was hurried, like that of a bullfighter whose sword has hit the shoulder blades and bounced out. The man was anxious to drive it in correctly the second time, and he swung quickly.

The hurriedness of it spoiled the aim, and he hit only a glancing blow. It went in, but it missed the gyrus of the brain and hit an artery. Pearson felt the hands twirl the electrode to see if it was in tightly.

Almost a thousand heads felt what he could not feel, the slow tearing of the artery and the soft seeping of blood into the cavity of the brain itself. Only a little of the blood went back up the tube, and the men were still unaware of it.

Only he and the Self knew that his death had begun. It would be a slow one, but not the most painful death he had ever had. Certainly, the tearing teeth of the killer whales and the infected harpoon wound that had taken two weeks to nudge him out of the body were more painful.

He was at peace; there was, after all, not so much to be disturbed about. Certainly, it would be uncomfortable out of the body, as it always was. And it would be a long wait. So many had perished the year before, and there were so few births, that it would probably be until the next series of births before he had a form again. Not that there was any pain involved in the between space, except the passive agony of not having pleasure.

And it would be cold too, he could feel that already. It was coming as surely as the blood was oozing out of the torn artery and puddling on the brain. Slowly, inexorably, like a tide coming in, the pool would build and build until it filled the fissure of his brain and began to build up pressure.

When the crevice was filled, it would begin to press against the different folds of the brain, shutting off more and more of the flow of blood to it, until the brain would begin to starve for oxygen and would begin to die cell by cell.

CHAPTER SIXTEEN

Kirby stepped quietly into His Excellency's private office and shut the door gently behind him. His Excellency sat with his elbows resting on the desk, his face cupped in his hands. He was asleep, Kirby was sure. Though he never slept more than four hours a night, he took frequent ten-minute naps, like a computer shutting down its inputs to analyze and cross-reference. Kirby waited a moment and then moved toward the desk.

He had taken two steps before His Excellency spoke. He did not lift his face out of his hands, and he seemed to be still asleep. "What is it?"

Kirby's jowls hung almost to his lapels; he approached the desk completely before speaking. He watched the man before him with tiny black eyes. When he spoke, he spoke solemnly; it was a habit with him. "Reports just came in from Dolphin Fleet."

His Excellency spoke from between his hands, as if he might get the business over without coming completely awake. "And . . . ?"

Kirby frowned; he did not like being treated like the butler come with some petty information about a visitor. He surmised that one day he would find it quite pleasant to put a bullet into the head that refused to look at him. It had been done before. "*Dolphin One* and *Two* report no disturbance, nothing unusual," he said.

His Excellency waited patiently. Kirby waited also.

Finally His Excellency gave a sigh and pulled his face out of his hands. He looked sternly at Kirby and shook his head. "Why do I always have to pull the information out of you a piece at a time?" He snorted and smiled; on the surface it was almost affectionately rueful; underneath, it was something different. It was always something different underneath.

"One thing I never have to worry about, Kirby: your being tortured into giving away state secrets. You don't even like giving your information to me. I'll bet they could cut off your eyelids and you wouldn't even give them your middle name." It sounded almost as if His Excellency were contemplating just such an act.

Kirby nodded solemnly. "A man in Security should always be discreet," he said stiffly.

His Excellency's smile opened like the jagged edge of a tin can. "Do you suppose you could subdue enough of your professional reticence to tell me what *Dolphin Three* has reported?" Even Kirby was never sure when His Excellency was engaging in a little playful mockery and when he was preparing someone for a roasting. It made them all a little uncomfortable, a little unsure of themselves, even Kirby.

"*Dolphin Three* reported everything operating normally, but they've been picking up blips every now and again, as if they're being shadowed by something. They don't know what, and it hasn't approached them." The words came out as if he were reading them.

"Captain Curry says everything's under control, and he only reported it because we ordered him to report anything out of the ordinary, no matter how trivial."

His Excellency looked steadily at Kirby. He seemed to be looking all the way down into his mind. Kirby resisted without moving. His Excellency spoke. "What's Curry like? You think he's just nervous?"

Kirby hesitated a moment before replying. He did so even when he knew exactly what he was going to say. It made most men think that he weighed every decision carefully. It made His Excellency bored. "Curry's not the type to come up with a lot of useless details just to look alert. Something must be out there or he wouldn't have mentioned it. Something out of the ordinary."

Almost a mile astern, four huge dark shapes bounced their ranging signals off the hull of *Dolphin Three*. More than a mile farther still, Longscreech bounced his ranging signals off them. Three hours later, the ship's shadows disappeared. Two hours after that, the shadows' shadow disappeared as well.

CHAPTER SEVENTEEN

Pearson stood frozen, the bottle tilted, the liquid still unpoured. The dolphin that he had become waited patiently in the glass box. The paralysis would not start until he was down in the pool again, but that would come too, creeping up his long body a muscle at a time until he would not be able to move his flukes, and then his peduncle. It would creep farther and farther up until his flippers became incapacitated and he would sink to the bottom to rest one, two, three, perhaps more minutes before awareness would fog up and slip past him, before he would slide on through to the other side and be between forms again, in the cold, dark, boring space between existences that everyone dreaded despite its transience.

Still, it was the periods in between forms that made the rest so deliciously sensual. Like a drink after a long thirst, the new body would taste better, feel better, move better than anything else within memory. He had forgotten how wonderful it was to be able to feel; he always forgot except when he was about to lose the ability or when he had just gotten back after a long absence.

He laughed to himself at how insatiable he had been when he had gotten back into the body after the massacre of Hummscreech's birth. Three years, three series of births without an opening for him, even with everyone making a child.

When he had finally gotten back into the body, he had rubbed himself on everything and anything that could not get out of his way fast enough, and he had almost driven the herd crazy with his demands for sensation. Clickwhistle had sung him for everyone once, and there was great merriment over preoccupation to get himself stimulated. For all the pain of losing the body to the teeth of the killer whales, the joy of the seasons that followed it made up for it, balanced it off. So many of them had been out of the body for such long periods that the water fairly churned with their love-making. And novelties were tried that even now were only rarely duplicated.

Only a nostalgia for coming back made it bearable to go out. He could not really complain; there were worse ways to lose your body if you had to lose it, and you always did, sooner or later. No sense to be mad at the humans when their clumsiness shook you out of the body like a hurricane. Anyone would have to admit they did not do it intentionally, nor did they revel in it like the sharks or their enemies. They simply did it, awkwardly, without intention or malice, but just as effectively and just as often.

The electrodes were scratching down through the tubes toward the surface of his brain. What a mixture they would be! Some parts of him twitching without either his consent or his control, a flash of rage, a sudden indescribable hunger, a bolt of fear, and a big, sharp, bright burst of ecstasy to be repeated over and over for the simple expedient of pressing a lever with his beak. He smiled to himself in anticipation. He would be a long time out of the body, and he savored the sensations that were coming. There would be a long, dull time when they would be all he would have of the sensation that a body could bring.

He ticked them off as they came: the thumping of his flukes against the case; the twitching of one, then the other, of his flippers; a few swallowing reflexes; a few bursts of boredom, annoyance, nostalgia; a few memories flashing as if they were happening again; and, interspersed, the accidental touching of a point that gave a sudden blinding insight into the meaning of everything, a sudden clairvoyance about a future life that would be duly mapped as "dead areas" in which no response had occurred. One wave of fear. He counted off each sensation as it came, according to the expectation Hummscreech had given him, waiting for the last flash, the one the men were looking for.

It came like breaking through the interface, a burst/slide of pleasure that tingled all his nerves at once and caused him to emit a supersonic burst of gratification that totally escaped his human manipulators. As an afterthought he remembered to whistle and move his head as a sign to them that they were in the right spot. He did it over and over again, modifying each motion so that it seemed to mirror what he was feeling so obviously that they could not miss it.

Still, it took them twice before they realized they were getting the very response they had wanted. Considering their dullness, twice was not excessive. He whistled and wriggled in the case again, splashing water out until they moved the electrode to hit just the right spot in his brain. Then he let it all flow through him and out, savoring it as it went, but passing it on to the others who waited to share his pleasure as well as his pain.

At sea, the whistling and clapping and erratic swimming, the leaping out of the water and slapping of flukes on the surface persisted as long as the current was on.

He waited patiently for the rest of it as the puddle

and pressure built up inside his brain. Fortunately, it was in a place where, though it would eventually interfere with his motion, it made no difference to his sensation. Just for an instant he felt what the pressure on his lungs would be like as he slid to the bottom of the pool, having given his last rising/falling cry for assistance.

The experience of losing the body was never one a dolphin could acquiesce to without a cry of distress, not for assistance but at least for company. He could hear the echoes of his own cry as it would rebound off the walls of the pool, and it disturbed him, not so much the dying as the dying alone. Of all the things the men outside the tank had done to him, isolating him was the worst.

Not that there would have been much purpose to having the others hold his blowhole above water a few more hours or a few days. The paralysis would get to the lungs before long, and no amount of holding him to the surface would do him any good then. Still, losing his body was a hard thing to have to do by himself, and it unnerved him a little. It was inescapable, he knew; what happened, happened. Still, he stared up at the men for consolation.

He fixed his eyes on the man on the far side, the man who had driven in the electrodes, and a shiver went through him as he recognized his own face.

Pearson dropped the bottle as he saw it and almost shrieked. The glass and soda splattered across the floor like a phosphorous bomb. He jerked back from the table like a dolphin exploding up out of the water and into the air. His legs went weak on him and he had to let himself collapse into the chair. He shivered like the dolphin in the tank.

For almost ten minutes Pearson resisted the argument mounting in his mind. Certainly telepathy was possible;

his own repetition of the legendary studies of J. B. Rhine had proved that. Certainly, too, the dolphins were an intellectual match for man at the very least. But the conclusion was just too hard to accept. Much more comfortable was the conclusion that he was hallucinating himself into a permanent schizophrenia. Intellectually, he inched his way toward the obvious; emotionally, he ran in the opposite direction. By the time he had begun to accept it, he was shaking with fear.

He walked slowly and unsteadily across the lab toward the far end of the room. The wooden door led into the observation room with its access to the hydrophones and underwater broadcasting setup. All that was useless now if what he hoped and feared was true. He walked toward the wooden door, but did not go through it. Instead, he turned to his left and pushed open the steel door that led to the pool, where Clickwhistle waited with fatherly patience.

CHAPTER EIGHTEEN

Clickwhistle and Longwhistle hung like inverted tear-drops in the center of the pool, sinking passively and then swimming slowly back to the surface to breathe again; they bobbled like plastic pool toys moved by the wind.

Clickwhistle opened both eyes in the darkened pool. The huge doorway that opened to the outer pool gave only a little light, blocked as it was from the moon by the balcony, and Pearson was not more than a broken blur through the interface, even when he had come as far as poolside. Even after the man had kneeled and clicked on the pool lights, he was no more than a colored image that broke up into laterally disorganized patterns as the water moved.

Clickwhistle increased the motion of his flukes without changing the angle of their stroke. His body ascended vertically out of the water like a ghost rising from the ground.

With almost the full length of his body out of the water, Clickwhistle pushed off his tail and arched into a graceful dive. As he passed into the surface of the water, he seemed to disappear completely.

Pearson started a moment later when the dolphin's head broke water a few feet from the edge of the pool. The dolphin's eye flashed at him, and the fixed smile seemed even wider. There were a thousand questions he wanted to ask, but he knew somehow that words would only get in the way, and yet he did not know what else to use. He groaned inwardly at his muteness.

For an instant, he felt the interface between water and air circle him like a belt. He felt the water caress his flukes as they moved languidly back and forth, and the sharp flat slap of the air as it dried him above the waterline. He heard the slow motion return of his echoes as they bounced off the steel door and the glass of the observation room.

He stared back into his own face through the dolphin's eyes, and, as he did, he almost pitched forward into the water. The gleam in the dolphin's eye was not his reflection but his own self transported there. He was looking at himself looking at himself.

A small terrified voice in him kept insisting on the alternatives; kept shouting "Hallucination! Self-hypnosis! Drug residual! Schizophrenic!" But it was a very small voice with no belief in what it said.

The dolphin dove again into the water, and Pearson felt himself carried along through the flood of liquid and through the echoes rebounding and spreading out like a net. He felt the smooth glide and the curving turn, and the long, quick flapping of the flukes that propelled him forward and then up out of the water.

He felt his skin dry a little in the air, only to be wet thoroughly again as he broke through the interface into the water. He felt the echoes of Longwhistle and the long sensuous glide of her velvet skin across his.

The inside wall of the pool loomed ahead of him and then swung away to the left just before the echoes had flattened out into straight lines where they impacted against the surface of the wall. He slipped through the turbulence he himself had created in the water; it had no effect on him as his skin wrinkled and compensated.

The doubled and tripled echoes of Longwhistle returned in a loud-soft, loud-soft beat as she moved slowly ahead of him. The pitch of the beat rose and then dropped as he caught up with her and swam parallel, touching her. Undulating together, they moved through the water like a single, two-halved body, until Pearson felt the pleasure about to burst from him. He felt her breasts bobble against him in the water and he realized that it was no dolphin who swam along with him and that it was not even the memory of the dolphin who had invaded his mind, but some kind of common memory of his ex-wife, something Sonny had communicated to all the other dolphins. He began to feel a pawn in some game the rules of which he could not even conceive.

He wanted to get back to shore, to get back into his own body; he wanted to un-know all that he already knew. He wanted to cry out to the dolphin to stop it, to erase his understanding. But there was no pulling free; he might as well have been a hamster in the hands of a research assistant bent on injecting him with truth serum for purposes the hamster could never imagine. He felt the arm swing over his smooth, shiny skin and a fingered hand caress his fin, as it had so many times before.

For an instant, he was back in his own body crouched at the side of the pool. And then, suddenly, he was back in the water, flashing out of the pool, across the narrow passageway into the outer pool. The water slid past him like a blur of scenery beside a speeding car, so that its nuances melted and flowed together, and the echoes came back so quickly that there was scarcely time to feel the pattern, except as a multileveled symphony of beats.

Up ahead, only a second away, he felt the ragged series of echoes that interconnected like a spider web of broken glass. They stood like an impact in the sound, shattering it and scattering the pieces across each other in a mosaic that spelled danger and death. The closer he got, the more jagged the sounds became until the echoes came back like knife points, piercing him, tearing at his ears and at his mind.

A mist of sound overlaid the jagged pattern where the spray of the last waves haloed the rocks. Sound tinkled back where the wave scattered itself up and over the sea wall and fell into the pool in rivulets down the fierce banks of jagged stones that rushed toward him in a crescendo of broken echoes like the points of teeth.

It was his turn out of the body, and his mind throbbed with the words he had been waiting seven years to hear, the words that triggered him toward the rocks. Pearson heard his own voice echoing, "They've turned it into a weapon!" In around it filtered Hummscreech's understanding of the whole, the larger scheme of things over which no creature had any control except to go willingly where he had to go and do joyfully what had to be done. In the last instant, Hummscreech let Sonny see the immediate pattern of things and a flash of what it would eventually lead to, although that was lost on Pearson as if Hummscreech were holding it back specifically from him.

As he burst into the air, the jagged network of echoes came back softened, in pastels of sound moving slowly because of the thinner medium, and he understood that he was losing his body to make a change in the human, not the one who had given him the courtesy of her affection, but the other one, the male who had blundered so many others out of the body.

The air patted at the skin more sensitive than a human eye, slid along its surface like a thinner form of water. But beneath him waited no tinkling splash through the interface and a second caress as the water rushed back along and over him. Instead there were rocks, jagged as knives, harder than anything he had ever felt, a danger even to brush against for fear of opening a cut in his delicate skin. Fiercer than even the teeth of a killer whale, the sea wall spread beneath him like an open mouth.

And the mouth snapped shut. The impact tore along him, opening him in jagged tears all along his side and underbelly; his head tore and his beak shattered along the lower mandible. Above his eyes, a gash opened in passing, and he slid over the rocks like wet flesh over a razor blade, until his head slammed against a second rock and blotted out everything.

He came out of it only momentarily, and his body seemed to be on fire, seemed to be coming apart in a thousand places, burning and tearing and shooting pain through him. Even with the rest of the Self absorbing much of his pain, he was an agony of cuts and gashes. Fist-sized holes had been torn in his velvet skin and down deep into the blubber that seemed to leak out like stuffing.

He felt rough hands trying to ease him off the rocks, felt them lift his head into the rough cloth of the lap. He looked up and said the words that had been the signal for him to make his leap out of the body. As he said them, he opened his eyes and stared at the curious creature who held his head.

The shock of seeing himself again, ten years younger, was like a body punch to Pearson. He had forgotten who he was, he had been Sonny for those few seconds and had lost completely his sense of himself as Pearson. The shock of recognition almost made him miss the last picture that faded out of Sonny's mind, a sharp clear picture of Cathy, diving nude into the pool like a dolphin herself.

CHAPTER NINETEEN

His Excellency let a little warmth creep back into his smile. "You're a very competent man, Kirby. You give good advice." The smile broadened almost into camaraderie. "Even if I do have to pull it out of you with hot pincers."

Kirby smiled solemnly. His Excellency looked at him steadily. "You're not comfortable about something," he said. Kirby almost frowned; that kind of intuition made him nervous. His Excellency went on. "Is there one of the three captains you think we should replace?"

Kirby shook his head. He had done the clearances on all four captains of the *Dolphin* Series; to admit that there was something wrong with one of them was to admit to error. There was no reason to admit to it, even if he could. They were the best men available. "No, sir," he said. "Flushing was the weakest link of the four, and even he was far superior to the fifth best captain in WESTHEM. I wouldn't replace them."

His Excellency gave his head a little shake of impatience. "Kirby," he said, "one of these days, you're going to drive me crazy making me draw everything out of you the way you do." He had a capacity for losing his patience without getting angry that disconcerted most men. Even Kirby was not quite immune to it. There was no sarcasm in his voice, and anyone who did not know him might have been tempted to take what he said next as a sort of personal joke. Kirby did not see it as such. "I know it makes you seem mysterious and powerful, Kirby, but it's a pain in the ass at times. Now tell me what the hell's bothering you."

"Yessir," he said. He did not make his usual contemplative pause. "It's that Pearson, I don't like him."

His Excellency nodded. "I don't like him much myself."

Kirby said firmly, "I think we should take him off the project."

"It's not a very important post," he said. What he was really saying was "Why should so trivial a detail be worth the attention of the head of the secret police?" Kirby was not answering. "Yessir," was all he said.

"Why do you want him replaced?"

"There's something strange in his file." Kirby frowned.

His Excellency eyed him like a snake hypnotizing a bird. Kirby resisted. "He had a wife," he said. "She left him."

His Excellency shrugged. "Common enough these days."

"We can't find her," Kirby said. His Excellency raised an eyebrow. Kirby went on. "If she were alive and in WESTHEM, my staff would know it. She got to the mainland by plane four hours after she left the Institute and checked into a beach-front motel. Then she disappeared."

"Disappeared?" His Excellency said. "From under surveillance?"

Kirby's words came slowly and falteringly. Even a ten-year-old mistake was painful to admit, especially when it should have become long since unimportant. "Pearson got government funds, so, naturally, he was under surveillance. But we were having a little trouble with one of our operatives then, and we got the report late. We got to the motel room about an hour after she arrived. All her clothes were there. The manager said he thought she might have gone for a swim. My men waited. She never came back."

"Drowned herself?" His Excellency asked.

Kirby shook his head. "Not likely. The currents are such on that part of the coast that a body would certainly have been recovered. We think she just vanished."

His Excellency frowned. "Does Pearson know?"

Kirby shook his head. "We conducted the investigation ourselves, so there was no report. He went looking for her after he got out of the crazy house, but after two weeks he gave up. It's a big hemisphere. I guess he decided she just didn't want to be found."

His Excellency nodded thoughtfully. "You think she's gone over to the other side?"

Kirby shook his head. "If she did, our operatives never got a ripple, and she wouldn't have been a prize worth the trouble to hush things up *that* secretly. That's what bothers me. She's just gone."

"You think the same people responsible for *Dolphin Four* have her?" His Excellency asked.

Kirby pursed his lips. "Could be. It's anybody's guess. If so, it could be quite a lever against Pearson. I think he should be taken off the project."

His Excellency nodded thoughtfully and frowned. "He's still the best man available. By rights, I should have made *him* head of that project instead of Rathgall."

Kirby frowned. "Rathgall's loyal, Pearson isn't."

His Excellency looked at the bulldog-faced man curiously. His eyes narrowed. "Why *did* you recommend Rathgall for that job?"

Kirby looked unruffled, but there were little beads of sweat on his forehead. He answered almost nonchalantly.

"My men checked him out; he's competent, and he'll follow orders. Pearson won't. Rathgall can be trusted."

His Excellency smiled slyly. "Don't tell me you trust somebody in this world, Kirby. I'm disappointed. I thought you were above human frailties like trust and fear."

Kirby smiled cynically and gave a little nod of his head. "I trust a great many people, Your Excellency—a little bit."

His Excellency nodded appreciatively. "Just the same, Pearson's the better qualified, even if he is a security risk. They're not likely to find anything anyway; the whole project is just one more shot in the dark. Besides, there's no worse treatment for people you don't like than to use them and then let them know they've been used."

Kirby knew it was a dismissal of his complaint, and he knew His Excellency thought it too trivial to pursue further. He knew it would make His Excellency angry not to let it drop. He pushed it anyway. "He could endanger the project, Your Excellency."

His Excellency shrugged. "Perhaps. But he's useful." There was an air of finality in his voice.

"He's not the scientist he was ten years ago." Kirby knew he had gone too far almost before he said it.

There was no particular malice in His Excellency's voice, and yet it let Kirby know he had said too much. "He stays," the man at the desk said.

Kirby nodded assent. His Excellency nodded and put his face back between his hands. He was already asleep when Kirby got to the door. Exactly three minutes later, he awoke and activated a small screen on his desk.

CHAPTER TWENTY

Pearson looked down into the pool; it rippled as if Cathy had just dived into it. But Cathy was gone. Sonny was gone. Only Sonny's feeling that her affection had been a courtesy, a social obligation any dolphin would have performed for any other, remained, and even the reality of that was fading fast.

The two dolphins moved soundlessly at the far end of the pool. Pearson squatted near the edge. Certainly, it was all a dream. He saw a broken image of himself in the water; the underwater lights and the refraction of the water made it strange and grotesque. His understanding broke and re-formed, broke and re-formed like the image on the water, a distorted picture, perhaps, but no hallucination.

He had made the first real interspecies contact, and yet he was not elated. Once, the thought of that kind of contact, even if he could have conceived of it, would have made his whole life worthwhile. Now it was only a nightmare of knowledge he wanted to escape.

He tried to resist the knowledge that had been in the mind of the dolphin, tried to ignore the purpose for which the dolphins had been sent. But it was no use.

For an instant, Pearson felt as if there were something huge sitting on his chest; something pushing the air out of him. No matter how hard he tried to inhale, he could not budge the huge weight that had settled on his lungs.

He could see nothing; nor could he emit a ranging signal to find out anything.

He could feel something soft yet solid under him. He felt air all around him, and he knew that he was on a hospital roll cart. He knew what to look for now, and he found it, halfway along his dorsal spine, a tiny pinprick in the continuous surface of his skin that meant he had been punctured by a hypodermic needle.

The weight that pressed on him like a mountain was his own weight, five hundred pounds out of the weightlessness of water. Every voluntary motion of his chest muscles was a day's worth of exertion, and his lungs filled and emptied erratically.

He could feel the chill of being out of the body creeping in on him, moving up from his tail toward his dorsal fin, but he could also feel his death coming as another move in the game of universe.

The cool night air blew in from through the opening to the outer pool, pressing his sweat-soaked shirt against him. Pearson tried to understand why, of all the things the dolphin could make him see, he chose those deaths. But he could no more understand it than he could understand why they had chosen him. He was already thought crazy by half the scientific community, and thought to be at least eccentric by even the favorable half. No one would ever believe what he had already learned, and Rathgall would have a field day with it.

Ten years before, at the height of his career, what he knew might have been given some credence, but now there was no chance it would even be listened to. Even his colleagues in parapsychology were not ready to accept it, despite their incessant demands for open-mindedness. If the dolphins had selected *him* to break the news of their intelligence to the world, they had certainly picked the wrong man.

There was an instant of being beside the pool again, and then he was upstairs on the balcony in the middle of a clear day, still wrestling with the decision to close the project, to put an end to the research. Every day, Sonny and the others seemed more human, perhaps even superhuman, and every day, the moral imperative to stop the research grew in him. Every day the practical part of him fought it.

There was little enough of the grant left for them to live on, even with most of the expenditures of the Institute suspended with the research. Some of it would have to be returned, and there was nothing of his own left; it had all gone into the project. There were, of course, research fellowships in other fields, or perhaps a teaching position, but they would not be able to start for months, and it would be a hard wait. What was more, he did not want to move away from the island, did not want to go back to the politics of the mainland.

And there was the problem of the dolphins. There were still five left, including Sonny, and there was no way to part with him. Certainly, Cathy would not hear of it, and he did not want to do it himself. Still, he was increasingly convinced that he had no moral right to experiment with them without their consent; no right to keep them penned up, no matter how much they seemed to treat it like a game and to enjoy it part of the time.

Cathy called from the opening between the pool, "John! Tessie's about to give birth!" He ran down the circular stairs and through the door to the inner pool. He followed Cathy into the observation room, and they watched through the underwater port as the birth commenced. Tessie floated, as if by intention, close enough to the port to make the birth clearly visible.

"That's odd," Cathy said.

He looked closely. "That's Lochinvar with her!" Pearson frowned. "A male doesn't assist in a birth."

"No," she said, "it should be another female. Gwendolyn was swimming around the pool with her just after the contractions began. I thought Tessie'd selected *her*."

They watched Tessie's stomach flex her entire body in one, then another, sharp spasm, and then contort herself almost into a question mark. The tail of the infant emerged first, and Cathy noted the time. A few more wriggling contractions and the baby slipped free and started its long swim for the surface and its first breath of air.

It had almost passed Tessie's head before they noticed something wrong. Instead of swimming below and behind the newborn and encouraging it to make for the surface, even helping it if need be, both Tessie and Lochinvar were swimming past it, on top of it, blocking its way to the surface.

They watched in horror as Lochinvar grabbed a fluke and dragged it toward the bottom, and Tessie punched the child's head downward with her beak. The baby wriggled, trying to free itself, but it had little enough time to get to the surface as it was and it was out of air. It thrashed almost free of Lochinvar's grip, but Tessie pressed her full body weight down on it and held it on the bottom until bubbles could be seen escaping from its mouth instead of its blowhole.

Pearson stared down into the pool for an instant before something grabbed his mind again and dragged him back into the water. Against everything in his nature, the dolphin that was Pearson took the fluke in his mouth and dragged the infant downward. He felt his sharp teeth catch in the fresh skin as the infant tried to pull free, but he held fast, despite all his instincts to let go.

He dragged the baby down as Clickfour pressed it toward the bottom of the pool. That it must die was beyond doubt; it was one more necessary step in the process of educating the human, though it grieved them both that whoever was being born should have to go back and wait again. They grieved for the long wait they were imposing on whoever had been born.

That they too, after three days of swimming in circles, would be dead as well of self-induced peptic ulcers did not concern them. That they too would have to wait in the dull, sensationless space between death and birth bothered them less than that they had committed someone else to an extended wait. They grieved for the unnaturalness of the act, but they could not escape it.

An absolute faith underran every action they took, as if they knew some basic premise of the universe that Pearson did not, as if they understood something so integral to existence that it did not even dawn on them that it could have escaped him. Pearson doubted that he would ever know what it was.

CHAPTER TWENTY-ONE

Kirby was still ten yards from the door of the Communications Room when the admiral stopped him. He gave the man a scowl like the striking of a blow. "What do you want, Hooker?"

The admiral looked at him anxiously. "What did he say?"

Kirby's frown deepened. "He said Pearson stays."

"What are we going to do?" There was almost a whine to it. The admiral seemed another species entirely from Kirby, and Kirby looked down his nose at him like a man inspecting a hamster. "*We* are not going to do anything. *I* am going to inform Rathgall, *he* will attend to it. *You* will do nothing."

The admiral looked up and down the hall and leaned conspiratorially close. "You don't think we'll have to kill *him*, do you?" He looked around as if they could escape surveillance if only he could spot the camera.

Kirby shook his head in exasperation. "Who? Pearson?"

Hooker plucked at his sleeve like a panhandler. "No, no," he said, "His Excellency. Cobbitt's ready but he doesn't have control of His Excellency's personal bodyguard. They're too spread out to kill all at once, and they're incorruptible."

Kirby pulled his sleeve out of the man's grasp. "Shut up! That's not to be discussed here." He looked around as if certain they were being monitored.

Hooker pursued him up the hall insistently. "But what if we have to act today? I need to know. I can't be ready at a moment's notice."

There was a cutting edge to Kirby's voice, and he used it on Hooker like a razor in the hands of a madman. "*You* don't have to know anything. If an execution is necessary, Cobbitt or I will handle it. You don't need to know anything except how to keep your mouth shut."

Hooker whined like a child. "I have a right to know; I put *Dolphin Four* where you wanted it. I'm in this as deep as you are. We don't have much time left."

Kirby looked at him as if weighing the possibility of killing him on the spot. He decided they might still need him to give orders to the fleet with His Excellency out of the way. "We have two full days if need be."

Hooker wheedled him. "Yes, but what about Pearson? What if they should contact him in some way?"

Kirby snorted. "*How? How* could they contact him? Ridiculous."

Hooker whined, "It isn't ridiculous. It's possible, and you know it, or you wouldn't be in such a hurry to get to Rathgall."

Kirby looked at the man with absolute disdain; he shook his head at what a poor species it must be to turn out such sorry specimens. Outside of His Excellency, the whole species was a sorry lot, and he would have to dispose of that specimen of human vanity and greed as well. He looked at Hooker as if he were about to hit him. Hooker took a step back. "If Pearson becomes a threat, Rathgall will be able to handle him. If His Excellency becomes dangerous, Cobbitt and I will see that he does not interfere. And if you bother me once more, two men will appear at a small private academy outside the city and blow off the back of a little girl's head."

Hooker went white with rage and impotence. "You wouldn't dare! I'd kill you!" He thrust his face almost onto Kirby's. The spittle of his rage flecked Kirby's jowls. Kirby sneered him back. One way or another, Hooker would not live out the week.

"You were told to stay away from here," he said sharply. Hooker glared at him through narrowed eyes seething with hatred. He plucked at Kirby's sleeve like a troublesome wart. Kirby yanked his sleeve away as if Hooker had contracted a loathsome communicable disease. "I don't want to see you here when I come out," he hissed, and walked away.

His Excellency raised an eyebrow at the act. The screen on his desk was too small to show all the details of the meeting, and they were both far enough from the nearest microphone for their conversation to be inaudible. Still, it was clearly a falling out of conspirators. His Excellency nodded solemnly to himself. Conspiracies were to be expected. Some were even to be encouraged. All were to be watched.

He watched Kirby go into the Communications Room without emotion. He waited ninety seconds before he pushed one of the buttons beside the screen.

CHAPTER TWENTY-TWO

The male dolphin surfaced near him and issued a series of clicks of different frequencies. Pearson was familiar with it from a hundred different dolphins, but he could never grasp it; nor could the computer they had attached to sort from it some meaningful pattern. It dawned on him finally why he had never been able to understand the dolphin language. The sounds were only half the language and they took their meaning, not from anything they represented, but from the experiences the dolphin was communicating telepathically. It was a kind of background music that gave the emotional key to how the pictures were to be interpreted.

Pearson's head drooped in despair; the clicks were utterly beyond him and it was too difficult to think in pictures, nearly impossible to clear the mind and focus on one single picture, one single experience, without running off in all directions, bringing in all the associations of the experience until he was a hundred overlapping impressions from where he began.

To Clickwhistle, Pearson's mind was a mind running out of control. Pearson seemed to babble incessantly about everything and anything, and his pictures were all interconnected and twisted out of shape by peculiar local customs and beliefs that made grotesque any recording of what he had experienced.

To Clickwhistle, Pearson had no sense of selection, no

ability to pick out one thing and stick to it; no attention span, like a very immature dolphin. Pearson was like the infants who had to swim beneath their mothers for almost a year until they got themselves oriented again to being in the body and stopped letting their consciousnesses run rampant trying to gulp down all of the sensation they had been missing for so long in the dark between space. He had none of the focus that allowed Clickwhistle and the others to get all the possible flavor out of their sensations.

Pearson's mind was inordinately strong, yet it was so erratic that the only way Clickwhistle could get anything into it was to take hold of the mind itself and draw it into his own and then force into it the experience it would need. And even then Pearson seemed to recombine whatever came in and to put it in new sequences and reverse it and thoroughly misunderstand it, especially when it got down to the basic, primary essences of things.

He seemed never to be able to put anything in its right sequence, and to Clickwhistle the sense of sequence was all pervasive. Yet Clickwhistle's concept of sequence was as unintelligible to Pearson as Pearson's concept of time was to Clickwhistle. Clickwhistle could go back into other experiences in the sequence, and sometimes, with the help of Hummscreech, he could go ahead in the sequence, but the sequence itself was immutable and immovable.

To Clickwhistle, all events of the sequence occurred simultaneously, and, occurring once, occurred forever; though everyone but Hummscreech focused on only a few events at a time in order to preserve the sensation of novelty. For Clickwhistle, all things had already happened, though he and the others moved through them one at a time, forward and backward, over and over again, like a child listening for the thousandth time to a story it knows by heart for the sheer pleasure of experiencing the words again and again.

Yet Pearson's mind worked as if there were things which had never happened before, and it seemed to combine and recombine every bit of sensation to work out what those things were. The mind seemed always in the process of re-creating the universe in a new way. To hold such a mind to a single experience took incredible effort, and despite his prowess, Clickwhistle was exhausted.

There was still so much to communicate and the time was so short that even Clickwhistle might have despaired of it had not Hummscreech said that it was something already accomplished. Yet what would come of it was not said, nor would Clickwhistle want it said. The game lay in playing blind man's bluff with the immutable sequence of the universe. To know how the game came out would ruin it, and Hummscreech would not do that.

Clickwhistle submerged and glided around the pool. He took a deep breath and went to the bottom and lay there relaxing. Longwhistle swam down beside him and hovered just beyond him, gently patting his head with her flukes. Focusing the alien mind was difficult, and the choice of what could be given it and what could not was harder still. But the choice of which things it could perceive and understand was the most difficult of all, especially since the mind seemed to have undergone a radical alteration.

Pearson lay back on the cement at the side of the pool and cupped his hands behind his head. He was exhausted. He felt like a two-year-old being dragged around a supermarket, tired and without any real understanding of what was happening to him, yet excited at the colors and sounds and smells. But there was so much of it, he could not put it together. Some subtle yet quintessential part of the pattern was missing.

No matter how he stretched his mind, it was still beyond him. The drug had opened him to sensation, but it had also taken away a lot of his ability to concentrate. He could see wholes with ease now, could see entire fields of data and the relationship of any one thing to all other things, but he could no longer see parts. His mind leaped in radicals of meaning, exponentials of understanding, but it could not stand still even for a minute.

Everything came up by the roots now, its associations still intact. There were no more single and separate ideas. Every sensation the dolphin put in his head was like the first split atom in a chain reaction. It was as if a machine programmed for analysis were feeding information to another machine programmed for pattern recognition. Everything spun him off onto ramifications and cross references, and by the time he worked his way back to the original data, the other mind was quantum jumps ahead of him.

Yet he knew what they had done was only the working out of a syntax of communication, a form that was as yet devoid of the content the dolphins intended as their real message. The thought that all of the incidents with the dolphins had been arranged intentionally ten years in advance, just so that he would have some common experience for them to build on, unnerved him. The thought of an understanding that could perceive things that far in advance and could arrange things so as to accommodate ten years' worth of change made him shiver.

It was more than just understanding the future—his work in parapsychology had prepared him for that; it was the power behind the understanding that scared him, and he pulled his mind away from the thought that even the incidents with his wife had been arranged.

He began to feel like a toy in someone's hands and he resented it. The more the thought edged itself into his consciousness, the madder he became. He remembered Cathy's report of how Sonny had used a ball to condition her not to fear his teeth, and he wondered how much of gaining her trust and then gaining her love was not arranged by Hummscreech.

He looked up at the grained polyfoam of the ceiling and shook his head. That was paranoid thinking, human thinking. Hummscreech did not control what happened, he merely saw it in its entirety and told some of what he saw. Whatever causes there were to the unfolding of the universe, they were beyond the powers of any creature in it.

"Is, is!" he thought. He had never really understood what the phrase had meant until that moment. Whatever happens happens because it has already happened. Nothing can change because it is already over. The sequence is fixed. The only thing that moved was awareness, and direction was a meaningless concept. From premise to conclusion, from conclusion to premise did not matter. There is no backward or forward within a complete circle, no cause and effect, no good or bad, just *is*, just the circle itself. He wondered if that was the secret the dolphins knew.

He hoped it was not. Closed systems were always intolerable to him, and the thought that he existed in one was unbearable. To have been led like a specimen a step at a time through an elaborate conditioning until he was ready for the kind of communication that they had in mind for him was humiliating, but to think that it was all part of a pattern that could not be changed made him angry and afraid. The powers he had met already made him feel vulnerable and helpless, and he was well aware of how his species would react to that feeling of vulnerability.

He thought of His Excellency and the other men who had sat around the conference table from him; not one of them could march in step with the music of another species, no matter how cosmic the beat. The day it became known that dolphins could control a human would be the first day of the war against the dolphins that could end only in the destruction of both species. Even if they had taken over the *Dolphin Four*, they could not hope to control all of man's weapons. Certainly, they could not believe that they could prevent man from triggering the destruction of all life on the planet in his frenzy, and surely they knew enough of man to know that destroy the planet was exactly what he would do.

For a terrible instant, he was afraid that they knew exactly that, and that they were proceeding through the whole unstoppable chain of communication, confrontation, and catastrophe because that was the way things were to happen and nothing could stop what was already done.

He felt like a puppet stumbling across a stage in the last act of a play so much beyond his comprehension that he could not even tell whether it was a comedy or a tragedy. And yet he tugged, however hopelessly, against his strings.

Pearson stood up and started to walk away from the pool. He had a vague idea of trying to leave the island, and a still vaguer idea that if he could not, he would have to kill himself. He wondered if they would be able to understand his suicide any more than he had been able to understand theirs. He wondered if he had correctly understood anything they had done to him.

Clickwhistle wondered if man's capacity for misunderstanding was infinite.

CHAPTER TWENTY-THREE

Pearson had not even started his second step when Clickwhistle burst through the surface of the water in a high leap. He clacked his jaws as Pearson had often seen older dolphins do to warn a younger dolphin away from something he was not old enough to manipulate or understand. It was both a sign of displeasure and a warning. Pearson ignored it and took another step toward the lab door.

He felt himself diving through the murky water of the mid-Atlantic, intent on a victim he knew to be just ahead of him. The echoes of his target had almost flattened, and there was no time for him to look to see what it was. The black shape entirely filled his field of vision, and he impacted at the dividing line between black and white.

No sooner had he hit than he veered away to his left, sliding past the huge wall of flesh that he had just hit. Too late, the head dipped and the teeth slammed together on the water he had just vacated.

He sped away from the creature and made for the surface. His lungs ached for air, and his blowhole broke the surface not a moment too soon. Fear and exertion had drained him, and he found himself exhausted already after only his second dive. He curled in the water and prepared to go down again. The huge body of the killer whale loomed below him.

Pearson saw through the eyes of the dolphin, but at

the same time retained his own identity. He was living the experience and watching himself live it at the same time. The part that thought as Pearson puzzled over the attack; for a dolphin to attack a killer whale went against all instinct. Yet he was doing it, attacking and waiting for another turn. To dive again meant less than a forty per cent chance of survival, and yet he was diving toward those deadly jaws and the huge teeth that lined them.

The head turned away toward its left side where it had just been hit by another dolphin as Pearson had completed his dive. He was at maximum speed when he hit, and the impact rattled his head, but not half so much as what he saw below them—the *Dolphin Four*.

He scanned it, looking for some clue as to what was happening, trying to match the configuration of men outside the vessel with the sequence of events on the tape. The inspection teams and the opened hatch indicated that the attack was only just begun. There was no indication from the mind of the dolphin as to why the whale was being attacked, but one thing was clear, they were attacking the whale, a suicidal mission at best, and they were doing it for some reason that could not be adequately explained without words.

Pearson understood that Clickwhistle was trying to give him an explanation of the event rather than the event itself. Clickwhistle knew he was failing. He had no words for what he needed to explain, and no pictures Pearson would be able to understand. He riffled Pearson's mind for an image to convey it, but it was like looking for one prop in a continent-sized theatrical warehouse.

When Pearson turned again, he saw the whale hovering over the vessel, but it had changed. The whale looked like a giant puppeteer, with heavy strings hanging down from it and attaching to different parts of the vessel. Most of them ran down into the hull through the open hatch, the hatch which opened wider as the huge beast jerked a string.

It looked ludicrous until Pearson realized its significance. The dolphin was apparently using the image he had just had about the dolphins making a puppet of him to tell him that the killer whale had taken over control of the ship.

He saw the inspection team move to the hatch and begin to close it. The whale dove without warning, the strings seeming to be contracted into him as he did. The inspection team never saw him coming, and in one pass the slashing head had reduced them to floating debris.

As the whale played out its lines of force and returned to its position, dolphin after dolphin dove to the attack until the whale's eyes closed and it began to sink to the bottom. As it did, the lines dissolved. The whale was dead and its power over the *Dolphin Four* was ended, that much was clear, but there was much that was not.

The whale fell slowly toward the submarine. Before it was halfway there, other killer whales appeared and ravaged the dolphins near the surface before forming a protective circle around the largest of their number who spun lines of force out of himself like a spider. The lines ran into the hatch and dispersed to attach themselves to different circuits. The rocket began to turn in its silo.

As it did, he saw the dolphins shove the body of the dead whale into the hatch. Pearson did not need to feel the flash that followed. He frowned as he pieced together what he had seen. Killer whales had attacked a submarine, dolphins had stopped them. But why? He still needed the *why*.

CHAPTER TWENTY-FOUR

Pearson felt the rough concrete under him, saw the pool beside him, then it disappeared. At first he thought he was back in the water, a dolphin again, but he was not, he was . . . somewhere else. He floated serenely in a liquid he could not recognize. Its viscosity even to his sensitive skin was something special. It was more liquid than water, and it had a good taste, one with nuance.

The liquid was at once colored and colorless, a thousand shades of color and yet clear, and it took him a while to realize that he was translating sounds and tastes into visual images. The liquid contained so many sensations that his senses began to overload. The liquid was as much thicker than water as water was thicker than air. It was the element his senses had originally evolved in.

He felt his mind break free and run cowering from the understanding that he was no longer a dolphin, that he was somewhere else than Earth in some form he could not imagine. But the fear lasted only an instant, before Clickwhistle enveloped Pearson's mind in his own. The experience intensified, and Pearson became aware of the liquid through all his senses at once; his whole being became a multifaceted sense organ immersed in a sea of sensation.

His ears picked up levels of sound that made even his dolphin sonar seem a kind of deafness. Sound moved

faster through the liquid than through water, and it came
on his ears like an echo chamber, except that it unified
things rather than distorted them. He felt every undulation of the liquid like the movement of his own skin,
which seemed to stretch forever.

He let his mind run along it, and he could feel the
tiniest vibration in it at what must be thousands of miles
away. He could feel others like himself moving in it also,
like two people under the same blanket, except it was
more like sharing a skin with a group of selves.

The slightest stirring enormous distances away stirred
him also, rippled his sensors, made him part of the movement itself. Everything was contiguous, everything was
connected, and there seemed no distinction between his
own body and the ocean, no integrity to his outer skin to
separate what-was-him from what-was-not.

He marveled at how big he really was, how enormous
was his skin, and how sensitive it was so far away. How
easy it was to be at peace when there was only Self and
nothing outside it. How easy not to move, and yet there
was no stagnation; a simple turn here or there rippled
the skin around his whole entity (could it really be that
many times bigger than Earth?). He had a kind of amoe-
bic consciousness that Self is All and All is Self.

He felt like a shell beyond which there was nothing
of importance. Inside the shell—but "shell" was too rigid
a word for it—were both sensors and sensations. He was
a complete world, both energy and the receptors of
energy, both feeling and what was felt at the same time,
the ultimate closed system, one that both produced the
sensations and sensed what it produced, an internal feed-
back loop, a closed loop whose perception of itself
generated itself in a continuous and unbreakable cycle.
The utter peace of it overwhelmed him, and he knew that

if he remembered this, nothing he could go back to would ever be enough again. He was the entity as its own environment. *Being* adapted to itself. Awareness of awareness. Instantaneous and indescribable. God digging his own body.

And then the body burst.

He was suddenly aware of something outside the Self, something negative, something monstrous and malevolent. He felt the intrusion of a force, an unreasoning hatred as pure in form as the pure form of the Self. An antithesis, the contrary to whatever the world had been that he had just been, yet so much larger than he had been, so much less varied but so much more powerful.

Pearson seemed to hang in space like a droplet of water on an enormous transparent glass, one tear-shaped drop of water the rest of which seemed scattered across infinity. He beaded like quicksilver dropped on a mirror, and the larger ball of which he had been a part spread out before him like a puddle in which splashed that force, that antithesis, scattering it like a cat ravishing a puddle, all menace and violence tearing at an illusive prey that disintegrated under its touch and reintegrated as a microcosm of itself, growing smaller yet larger with each blow.

Paroxysms of destruction splattered the Self and scattered the integrity of the being of which Pearson had just been both part and whole. The parts dispersed, and the force that had split them expanded in pursuit.

In all directions, microcosms of the Self spread outward from their old integrity into space with the dark force pursuing them, the active tiring itself against the passive. The expanding pushing meaninglessly against the yielding. Scratching uselessly for purchase against evanescence. The malevolent futilely scattering the joyous; both knowing, even as the dark drove the light outward, that the cycle would turn again, that the Self would come crowding back in on the force that drove it outward now, helter-skelter away from itself. When the Self had been dispersed to the ultimate, the universe would begin to reassemble itself and the Self would start rushing back together, pushing it, imploding it, until it too was forced back into a static ball within the ball that had been all there was.

Pearson drifted across space, a part of a part of something huge, something unfathomable driven outward by something seemingly more huge and even more unfathomable. Each piece, a microcosm of the whole, each piece like a piece of DNA able to reproduce itself, carrying in itself all that would be needed to reassemble the whole.

There was neither remorse nor despair in the expanding entity, being driven apart, seeking a form across the long, dark sensationless void. He tried to think where he had felt that trip before, that dull monotonous time between sensation and sensation.

Suddenly it became clear to him, not the phrase but the meaning behind it, not clear in any intellectual sense but understanding which knows without even knowing that it knows. A knowledge that knows, by existing, what it is. "Out of the body" was not merely out of the dolphin form but out of the original body with which he had been one for a few moments that were perhaps eternity.

"Out of the body" was the longing to return to cohesion, to be back together, to regain integrity, become an entity again. It was a longing that was more poignant in that dark, cold space between one form and another.

The thought kept slipping away like mercury running through the fingers of his mind. Even with the help of the intelligence that was hiding on his planet, he could not hold the thought in his consciousness for long. It was an understanding he would never really have, an experience he could only vaguely comprehend, like a dog given a few moments in a man's body. He perceived only the shadow of the shadow of it.

The cohesion of the entity eluded him, though he dimly perceived a sense of absolute integrity from the minute particle of the Self that had become the dolphins. How a thing could be dispersed and yet remain whole was beyond him, and much as he struggled, the contradiction kept resolving itself first one way and then the other, never capable of keeping the equilibrium that was understanding. That sense of oneness was a miracle beyond comprehension or articulation.

The longing to feel that oneness would pursue him forever and poison his days. He seemed so far removed from it already that he saw only the penumbra of a shadow, too faint to perceive, too precious not to try. All he could sense was the fading ghost of something, something forever beyond his grasp, an absence worse than death. An absence of oneness with the Self was torment worse than utter darkness. It made Pearson want to die.

CHAPTER TWENTY-FIVE

Clickwhistle felt the mind slipping from him, tearing itself free of him to plunge into nothingness; intentionally, insistently, willing itself, not merely out of the body, but out of existence. It was hard for Clickwhistle to conceive. He had tried to show the creature the beautiful thing, the harmonious thing that allowed them absolute optimism.

He had shown the creature the faith-giving, sustaining memory of Home, of how it had once been and would be again, and he had sung it and formed it perfectly, beyond anything even he had ever done before, drawing the quintessence of it out and making that stand alone; refining it so that the pure essence of the experience was there unadulterated, unavoidable, the pure joy of Home and the joy of being.

And the creature had totally misunderstood the whole thing!

Clickwhistle's mind boggled at how the creature could so totally misconceive the thing as to want to cease to exist because of it. The human capacity to distort the fundamental was astounding.

That what he had done so perfectly and beautifully could have become so perverted in the creature's understanding so stunned Clickwhistle that he almost let the mind slip from him. He could feel his own body slipping down into the water. Focusing the mind left him no strength to maintain his own position, and he could feel himself sinking. He would have to let go soon or he would drown.

He felt his blowhole close automatically as it passed below the surface. The power in that mind was a match for his own, only its lack of co-ordination kept it from pulling free. Had Pearson been able to focus his force on his own death, he would have pulled himself from Clickwhistle's grasp like a hand leaving a glove.

For the first time, Clickwhistle was grateful that the mind could not discipline itself, could not make coherent its own force. Concentrated on a single direction, the force of that mind would be overwhelming. Potentially it had a vigor, an energy, that even Clickwhistle stood in awe of. Clickwhistle had not realized before how strong the mind of the creature was; more strong even, than it was distorted. It was a match in pure power for the force that hounded them, and for an instant Clickwhistle could see a little ahead, not like Hummscreech, but ahead enough that he knew he could neither let himself sink nor let the human mind pull itself free.

Yet he felt himself sinking. For an instant, the mind felt strong enough not only to propel itself through the interspace between being and nonbeing but to drag him along with it. For just a flash, Clickwhistle felt a touch of human fear. For sheer force, the mind was superior even to his own. For raw power, it was astounding. Had it a capacity to focus itself, it would be truly cosmic in its scope.

But it could not focus itself. The difference between its natural force and that of Clickwhistle was the difference between ordinary white light and the coherent light of a laser. For all the incoherence of its energy the light of the human mind was still blinding. But its brightness began to fade with Clickwhistle's air.

Clickwhistle felt himself begin to rise in the water. He could not spare enough of his attention to see what lifted him but he knew anyway. It was Longwhistle, coming up alongside him, hooking her flipper under his and lifting him toward the surface where he would be able to breathe again. He would not sink again, not if it took all night now. Longwhistle would hold him up, treading water for both of them, while he used all his strength to drag the mind back from its headlong rush into death.

The absolute despair of the mind was a drain on Clickwhistle. There was no way to resist its power, and it took most of Clickwhistle's strength just to maintain contact with it. If he did not soon find a way to divert it, to deflect it onto some other track, it would plunge into the abyss of nonbeing, dragging him with it. Clickwhistle strained to shape in the other mind the image of the force that pursued them across the universe. Only *that* had focused the power of the other mind as much as the experience of Home. It triggered in the other mind something Clickwhistle could not quite understand—rage. He relied on that and sang.

The ability to willfully die made him immortal; there was nothing left to fear now, the worst had already happened and everything else was simply a matter of relaxing. In relaxing, he was like an idiot's hand, closed in an impregnable fist because it is closed without intention. His was the force stronger than death. Caring for nothing, he was suddenly master of all.

He could feel himself pulling his mind slowly out of the grasp of the dolphin. It could not stop him; nothing could stop him. Vast reservoirs of power had been freed, and they flowed out of him like a mighty river, carrying him toward nothingness. He could feel oblivion yawning before him, an empty unfillable void. Yet compared to the emptiness inside him, it was nothing.

Just before he passed into it, the void became a mouth, a mouth of pure malevolence, wider and deeper than oblivion, the mouth of the entity that had dispersed the perfect world for which he longed. Its breath was the breath of death, and its touch turned his despair first to revulsion and then to rage. Even more than he wished to cease, he wished to strike one blow, however fruitless, against that being.

Clickwhistle felt the mind bolt in another direction with such force that his own mind was almost thrown loose from it. The mind jerked him forward like a huge dog dragging its master on a leash. There was no stopping this force, this rage, equivalent to the malice that pursued.

It lacked only a focus for its attack, and Clickwhistle knew what that focus was intended to be.

CHAPTER TWENTY-SIX

There were only two men on duty at that time of night, and Kirby told them to wait in the hall. They obeyed without question as they always did. He put through the call himself, sitting at the console like a man staring into a crystal ball. The fat face appeared on the screen as if it had been there all the time and had needed only Kirby's touch to make it visible. His Excellency had intercepted the image almost a half second before; Kirby did not notice the delay. His Excellency recognized the tiny black eyes almost immediately. The bulk of the man seemed to clog the whole of His Excellency's small desk monitor.

Neither man wasted time on amenities. Rathgall spoke first. "What happened?"

Kirby shook his head. "He said no."

Rathgall nodded. "Why?"

Kirby shrugged. "I don't know. He thinks better than the rest of them; I can't tell. Subtle, you know? Not characteristic of the species at all."

Rathgall frowned. "You think he might be one of them?"

Kirby scoffed at the question. "Of course not. But he could be dangerous just the same. What about Pearson?"

"I don't think he'll be much of a problem. He looks like he's having another breakdown. It wouldn't take much to push him in that direction."

"Do you think they could contact him?"

Rathgall shook his head. "No. If they could, they would have done it before now. I think they tried during his research and failed."

"Just the same, I don't like him around them. How long can you keep him from getting specimens?"

"He has them," Rathgall answered curtly. He seemed to anticipate Kirby's reaction.

"How the hell did he get them? I thought they were stopped in transit."

"Those were, the plane crashed. Some fishermen caught these locally. One of his assistants got them before I could stop it."

"I don't like it. It's too coincidental."

Rathgall nodded agreement. "True. It's probably an attempt to contact him. What do you want to do?"

Kirby pursed his lips. His studied pause stretched out into real contemplation. Finally, he spoke. "Kill him."

Rathgall smiled slightly. The points of his teeth glistened just under his lips. "When?"

"As soon as possible." He paused, thinking of His Excellency. "Make it an accident."

Rathgall nodded solemnly. "He'll probably sleep late tomorrow. He's used to working late at night. I should be able to get him here around lunch. My sharks should be hungry again by then." He smiled broadly as if an idea had just struck him. "Of course!" he said, "we'll have him for lunch!" He laughed, genuinely pleased at his pun. Kirby was not amused. Neither was His Excellency.

"Don't waste any time. Hooker's weakening. I may have trouble waiting until the time is right."

Rathgall frowned. "Can you move the ship without him? It's a big ocean. It could be hard to find otherwise."

Kirby shook his head. "Even *he* can't move them now. Only His Excellency can."

"Maybe we'd be better off without him."

Kirby shook his head. "No, with His Excellency dead, we'll need Hooker to give the command."

Rathgall nodded his understanding. "When?"

Kirby shrugged. "There's no need to hurry if your affair with Pearson goes all right. Unless Hooker cracks, we can afford to wait a couple days."

Rathgall nodded. "I'll call you back tomorrow afternoon with the unfortunate news about Pearson."

Neither man said good-by. His Excellency's screen went blank a second after Kirby's, and he switched to the corridor outside the Communications Room. When Kirby came out, Hooker was nowhere around. His Excellency followed his chief Security man all the way back to his room on the monitor. Satisfied Kirby was asleep, he deactivated the screen and sat back. If he was angry, not a gram of it showed on his face, even in the empty office.

CHAPTER TWENTY-SEVEN

Pearson waited as the picture formed within his mind. When it was complete, he felt himself begin to form within the picture. The drop that was the Self sped through empty space, traveling endlessly outward from the pursuing force, until it slowed and hung above the Earth like some detached piece of the planet's liquid come home again after a long fruitless journey.

It hovered there, and Pearson hung suspended both in it and outside it at the same time. Outside it, he saw it hover like a spaceship over the face of the deep like the ocean's own reflection staring back down at it. Inside it, he became, not part of the drop, but the whole of it.

He felt the same continuity of being he had felt before, the same boundarylessness that he had longed for. He was again a single entity; smaller perhaps, but no less complete. He had the same endless möbius strip of skin, indivisible yet communal, a skin packed with other parts of the Self as if the whole inhabitance of that large bubble had been packed into this one drop to escape. Like a hologram, each particle contained the whole, infinitely divisible yet without division.

Though the understanding of it was beyond him, he could feel the completeness of the organism of which he was again a part. All the entities that had originally been within the world/organism were still there, though the liquid itself was no more than a cell of the body that had been. Like genes within a cell, each entity traveled within every transparent waterdrop of the Self that moved through every section and direction of the universe.

Like cosmic DNA, the globe floated complete in itself, self-generating and potentially, when it was time, capable of regenerating the whole organism again. Within the envelope of liquid, as if on command, he felt each entity activate itself and move slowly into a physical form, congealing slowly into a finite number of creatures he immediately recognized as dolphins. He felt his own essence bend and solidify into the vague approximation of its original shape, and then the bubble broke, spilling the dolphins out into the sea like a seed pod breaking and scattering its own essence on the wind. They fell like molten drops of metal, hitting the surface of cold water and congealing instantly into permanent shapes. By being, Pearson understood the dolphin smile.

And yet from beyond, he could feel the fringes of something else, the first finger tips of something feeling blindly for them in the dark of the void. He could feel it come like wisps, like tiny tendrils spreading out to investigate an area into which to expand. He felt it like the first stringy fragments of fog grow, until it hovered over the ocean like a dark billowing thunderhead. He felt it hang lower and lower over the ocean, as if trying to peer into it to see what form they had assumed. Then the cloud, like the waterdrop before it, congealed and split, dropping into the water new forms, new intelligent life, killer whales, dropping from the cloud like stomachless mouths.

Far fewer than had dropped from the bubble of the Self, but with an appetite equal to all who fled before them in the water. As he fled, Pearson became aware of an incongruous sense of play, of children scattering before the one who is "It." He felt, coming back to him from the others, a kind of delicious terror, serious and yet fun, that he could not share, no matter how closely he came to being one of them.

The malevolence splashed into the water almost behind them, but it then had already dispersed and it pursued them with a lessened vigor. He sensed a limitation on the power that pursued them in their new environment, as if by entering a physical form it had lost many of its prerogatives and much of its power. Something had mollified the threat, something that he could not understand, and perhaps never would.

He had a flash of dolphins swimming in a herd with whales coming in behind them, all mouth and teeth, always just a little too late as the dolphins scattered as if they could feel it coming.

Pearson saw the dark spaces between the stars. He flashed a vision of the dolphins dispersing into space and a vision of what waited for them between the stars. He felt the force in the dark spaces expand like hunger, and he began to understand who had triggered the *Dolphin Four* and why.

CHAPTER TWENTY-EIGHT

Clickwhistle splashed water up onto Pearson and took off on a slow turn around the pool. He was exhausted; it was like holding back a tide to control the force in the human's mind. He could feed it experience, but there was still no way to control his understanding. Though he was sure the man understood parts of what he was shown, he felt the human had missed the essential, underlying premises of the game, had perhaps not even understood that it was a kind of game.

Longwhistle glided smoothly along with him, drafting, then moved ahead of him so that he could draft on her wake like riding the bow waves of a ship. They glided around and around the pool while Pearson tried to make sense out of what he had experienced. Clickwhistle made no further attempt to enter his mind for a while; it would have taken all the strength he had just to hold on while the mind processed and digested, made erratic associations and cross-referenced everything until it was a muddle no dolphin could sort out.

The very process of Pearson's thought would have been a grueling experience for Clickwhistle, like being exposed to a very loud noise for a long time. The reverberations of each thought were amplified and interconnected in endless associations. Much as he admired the power the mind had, he felt a slight distaste at its inability to focus itself. The whole of the contact was an ordeal.

Clickwhistle

Clickwhistle let himself rise slowly to the surface and slept, dozing for a few seconds as he sank and then propelling himself to the surface again to breathe. It regenerated him, but he could not afford to do it for too long. He could not let Pearson alone with his thoughts for very long or he would be light years of reasoning away from where he was needed. He would be lucky to get him back at all if he waited much longer. He swam reluctantly to the edge of the pool. The ordeal had to be begun again, but what was to be conveyed was something only Hummscreech knew; Clickwhistle would know it only as he passed it on to Pearson.

He eased into Pearson's mind, letting himself come to grips slowly with the churning mass of energy that was a human mind. It was like a man reaching gingerly into a cement mixer to extract something floating near the surface.

If Pearson's mind had been a whirlpool before, it was a maelstrom now. Everything churned and overlapped, mixed in and blurred together, until to Clickwhistle it was a meaningless smudge. He wondered if the man had understood anything. Hesitantly, he slid his mind between the energy and the experience and focused one on the other.

Pearson swam in a primordial sea, hot almost as soup. The thick soup seemed alive with things, and the thickness was a pleasant reminder of the thicker though infinitely more enjoyable liquid of the Self. He dozed near the surface, bobbing up and down at intervals to breathe as Clickwhistle had just done.

The thick water massaged his skin and lulled him into a state of relaxation that resembled sleep. Everything was so plentiful and there seemed so much time, so much play ahead; everything seemed so much like Home, which waited at the return end of eternity.

Visions of Home glided through his consciousness, filling him with great pleasure as he floated far enough from the herd to be alone but close enough not to be lonely. He swished his tail languidly like a fan over a tropic emperor and moved lazily upward toward the interface. Every once in a great while, he sent off a ranging click to see that he had not drifted too far from the rest.

The single characteristic he carried like a gene was the ability to appreciate solitude, not to prefer it, but to live comfortably away from the rest of the Self for a time. So long as he was in the body, the Self could tolerate, even enjoy, its own dispersion.

Until he felt the teeth puncture his flukes, he had no idea that the killer whale was there. The pain was intolerable. The teeth punched through the delicate outer skin, and all but interlocked below the surface. He jerked down against the bite and thrashed his upper body in an effort to free himself, but it was too late. Although the pain was excruciating, he could not pull free. The killer whale was locked onto him, closed like a sharp vise on his tail, crushing and tearing his delicate flukes so that even when he let go there would be no escape.

Pearson felt a streak of terror whiz through him. There was going to be no escape this time; no near miss to scar a peduncle or a flipper or a stretch of skin that thickened and became insensitive and seemed like a hole in the body the rest of the cycle. With the first searing twist of his body, he knew it was all over, but still he wrenched himself to his right, twisting as he did.

The second whale hit him from the side as he turned his stomach up in his attempt to twist free. A whole side of him seemed to have been torn away. They hit like sharks, tearing not swallowing whole as they did to feed. The second driving tear from the other side made it inescapably clear that they were killing for pleasure, not for food, killing to fulfill the necessity that drove them through space after the Self. Systematically mutilating him, the fifth slammed into him like a ship ramming a dock and tore a huge hole in his side from his flipper back toward his tail.

He no longer struggled. This was the end of it, and there was no longer any reason for struggle. Any chance he had was long gone, and to struggle would just make his agony longer. Another whale hit him from the left, and he felt his left flipper being torn away.

Turning his head slightly and moving his left eye back and down, he saw it slide out of the whale's mouth and float like a jagged flat rock toward the bottom. Without realizing it, he had been screaming the dolphin distress call ever since the first strike.

Not that he expected any help, but it hurt less to call out, and it had probably given the rest a warning to escape. There was no way of coming to his rescue without sacrificing the whole herd, and it was not expected. Certainly, it is a hard thing to say good-by to someone even if you know you are going to see them again before too long, and it was no less easy to die as a dolphin and bid everything farewell again.

He barely felt the next two strike him like huge knives, using their teeth, not to hold as usual, but to tear, to mutilate and destroy. The fangs sank five inches deep into his side and carried away with them a huge chunk of his flesh. His blood had long since clouded the water around him, and the taste of it was by now apparent to every dolphin within five miles in the direction of the tide.

The taste of it almost drove him into frenzy, and he

thrashed his body to pull himself free. But the pincers of the whale held his tail fast and he could not move himself. Much as he tried to convince himself that it was only a temporary thing, the panic grew in him. Cessation frightened him; not the pain, but the absence of sensation.

The panic escalated and he thrashed more and more wildly to escape. But the whales held him fast, and though he could not tell it, he was much too far gone to swim away even if they left him go. He was, for all purposes except his own, already dead.

The whales tore at him with a cold, mechanical fury that was pure, impersonal malice. They moved precisely, not one ever getting in the way of his colleagues; not one ever missing his turn; not one failing to open a new gash on a body that had already lost most of its unbroken surface.

There was a hard slap of the flukes against his face, and his lower jaw all but disintegrated. He slipped toward unconsciousness, fighting desperately to avoid it even at the price of more pain. But he could not avoid it forever, he felt the next hit, and then he was totally alone, more empty than he had ever been; colder, more desolate, blind, and numb, unable to hear or feel or taste, able only to be aware of the slow passage of time.

Darkness, coldness, loneliness, not characteristics but quintessences.

CHAPTER TWENTY-NINE

Pearson's consciousness hung suspended, motionless; not Self, not dolphin, not man. There was nothing to do but wait; and nothing to do while waiting. And he waited. Seemingly forever. And then he waited more. Slowly, like a numbness, something worse than the cold and the dark and the loss of sensation began to creep in on him—boredom. It stretched the time out and made it an agony of dolor. He tried his memories, but the real sensation had faded, and all he could approximate was a place and an event but nothing that could really be felt.

The time dragged so slowly it seemed to have stopped, to have turned to stone. He continued to wait. He was out of the body, and he remained out seemingly forever. Nothing came, no new awareness. Things went on and on. Nothingness went on and on, worse than nothingness because nothingness at least has no sense of itself. His time out of the body went on and on and on and on and on endlessly in the same monotony. Eternal sameness. Space without motion, without time.

Then suddenly the darkness changed.

There was still little to sense and less to sense with, but things were growing, he was growing, and soon he felt conscious of a form, a physical self again. A low throbbing permeated his liquid world, his easy flowing gelatin world. It did not offer much, but after the total emptiness of being out of the body, it seemed a feast of sensation.

Clickwhistle

His tail broke out into the water first, and the chill of sensation it sent through him was almost worth the eternity out of the body. He felt the interface between his mother and the water with an exquisite sense of contradiction. Finally his head slipped free and he passed out of one world into another through a gate of flesh. Everything he had ever felt poured over him as he slipped into the water like a launched ship. Behind him the gate closed silently.

The overwhelming sensation was almost unbearable after so long without any. He wanted to feel everything at once; his eyes, ears, tongue, skin seemed all empty and crying out to be filled. He waved his flukes and rose like an elevator to the interface, where his forehead broached the surface and he sucked in the cool air above it. His tiny lungs filled like a purse.

Slowly, his body grew longer and stronger and more mature until it rode easily and confidently on the outer fringe of the circle around Hummscreech.

In Pearson's dolphin mind, Clickwhistle's song formed the image of killer whales and of the rest of the entity, which crouched between the stars waiting impatiently for a chance to strike. He watched a part of the thing that had pursued them transform itself into the killer whales, which hunted them constantly through the primordial water, and he saw that form molt again, into another shape, not a shape of the water but one of land, a thing with two legs that had only begun its long cycle of mutation and growth toward the technology that would eventually be able to drive the Self from its sanctuary.

He watched parts of the Self molt as well and shed their dolphin forms like old skin to sink also into the ragged form of man, to dwell in it until the dolphin form and even the Self faded from memory down the long centuries. He felt the amnesia that would grow in those of the Self go into voluntary exile, and he felt the poverty of sensation that would wall off their identity like a scar, immune even to pain.

Clickwhistle felt the mind try to break free, to smash its way through the force that held it and filled it with memories it did not want to have. But he did not let go; there was more to be sung of the song he himself had forgotten so long ago.

Pearson tried to pull himself out of the image in which he was immersed. Not even the contentment of belonging again was enough to pay for the understanding that went with it. He did not even have to hear Clickwhistle sing the identity of the ten who, when they next went out of the body, would not return to it for a long, long time. He knew he was one.

CHAPTER THIRTY

Pearson found himself again at the side of the pool. He could see the first hints of gray in the sky through the doorway to the outer pool. It had been a long night, longer than any he would ever have again. He tried to calm himself, to work out an explanation to disprove what he already knew to be a fact. Perhaps the dolphin had meant something else; perhaps he was again misunderstanding everything. Perhaps he was not meant to identify himself with the dolphin in whose body he had experienced so much. He had, after all, shared the consciousness of the other dolphins during the night and that had not meant that he . . . It was impossible to believe.

How could he be, not only an alien species disguised as a man, but an alien creature disguised as a dolphin disguised as a man? How could he have his own set of incarnations stretching back behind him as the dolphins did behind them! And if it were true, to what end had they finally come to wake him from his forgetfulness?

He refused to look into the pool; to look into the pool would be to see himself. His heart beat as if it would never slow down, and his head throbbed. For an instant, he thought that perhaps he was about to die and that this revelation had come to him because his long exile in human form was about to end and he was to be welcomed back to his true family. He half hoped that they had come to collect him for the long trip home again. But he knew that was not so, that the flight outward would go on for a long, long time before it reversed itself.

Though he could not yet adapt to it, he had already begun to accept that he was not on his home planet, not even in his home body, or even in the body they had adopted on coming to this planet at the edge of a minor galaxy, but he balked at what the acceptance meant.

For it to be true meant that none of his life was real, none of his joy or sorrow anything but an act. It meant his whole identity was a fake, a disguise to conceal him until it was time for him to act. And now it was time. The intuitive leap that had carried him to his true identity before Clickwhistle had sung it could not quite carry him to what he was meant to do now.

He knelt finally at the edge of the pool and looked down through his reflection. Clickwhistle lay on the bottom, resting; Longwhistle floated just above him. Pearson wondered for an instant if Cathy were also one of the dolphins. Certainly, it would make more sense of what had happened between her and Sonny. Was that why she had left without saying a word, because she knew? Was she too part of the awakening of John Pearson? He wished he could ask Clickwhistle the questions, but he knew that only Hummscreech would remember the answers, and they were things it did not apparently suit the universe for him to know.

Clickwhistle rose slowly to the surface, the female dolphin moving with him like a shadow. He seemed to move more from her power than from his own. He had barely enough strength to get to the surface. It had taken a long time to waken his brother, and he was exhausted.

Still, he forced himself to contact the other mind again. It was a maze of countervailing ideas and directions. It jumped every microsecond from thing to thing, flitting from one question to another so fast that Clickwhistle could not keep up with it. The total chaos of the mind was appalling; it was like being permanently dizzy, constantly in motion without clear reference points.

Every time he entered the mind, it was like stepping into the middle of an explosion. And to take hold of that energy and try to channel it was an enormous, backbreaking task. Certainly, there would be no resistance now, but he hoped for little in the way of help. Pearson simply could not keep his mind still, no matter how much he might like to co-operate, and it would be a while before he would be able to do so.

Far from making it easier to control the mind, the new knowledge had made the mind a turmoil of conflicting arguments, most of them carried out in words and in so scattered a fashion that Clickwhistle could only guess at what was going on. At best, he could isolate pictures here and there, but even those were so interconnected with other thoughts or so double exposed that most of them were indecipherable. Clickwhistle let it all run by him in despair for a moment and then again slipped over Pearson's mind.

Pearson floated in the murky water of the mid-Atlantic. Below him sat *Dolphin Three*. Pearson groaned even before he saw the familiar dolphin beside it and the unfamiliar one on the other side of it. He did not even have to be shown himself inside it.

Clickwhistle had dropped below the surface before Pearson started to yell. He let the mind go with satisfaction and surfaced across the pool, but Pearson did not see him. He was too busy shouting into the water. "How the hell am I going to steal a submarine??!"

Clickwhistle

By the time Pearson lay back in complete exasperation, Clickwhistle was already dozing near the surface. Longwhistle floated next to him just in case. Pearson did not even remember going to sleep.

CHAPTER THIRTY-ONE

The sun was bright through the doorway at the far end of the pool when Baker and Fallow entered. They found Pearson sprawled by the side of the pool and rushed to him. Baker rolled him over anxiously, and Pearson blinked himself into consciousness. He frowned at Baker without recognition. The man seemed unclear to him for a moment; the only thing that was clear was the answer he had been seeking when he had fallen asleep.

"Are you all right?" Baker asked, helping him to his feet.

"What are you doing down here?" Fallow asked before Baker had finished.

Pearson ignored both questions and answered with a question of his own. "What time is it?"

"Almost nine o'clock, why?"

Pearson cursed. Every minute counted now. "Where are the keys to the Rover?"

Fallow fished out the keys. Pearson did not wait to ask him a second question; he grabbed the keys and headed for the opening to the outer pool. Clickwhistle and Longwhistle were dozing near the surface as he passed.

The tires screeched as Pearson wheeled the Land Rover around in the driveway and slammed into second as it straightened itself with the roadway. Clickwhistle let his head rise out of the water for a moment and then let it slip back under. He had earned his rest, and his brain ached. Even Pearson's movements were like an explosion.

Pearson turned right at the end of the driveway and sped down the coast, covering the eleven miles to Point St. George in a little over ten minutes and cursing the Land Rover for not being a sports car. He parked at an angle in front of the low Administration Building; the pool was in a long building behind it.

Rathgall would already be at work in the pool. Unlike Pearson, he did not do his best thinking at night but rather in the prosaic light of day. By now, he might even have finished one of the experiments he had mentioned. Pearson pushed through the glass door of the Administration Building and down the long corridor. The receptionist's desk was empty, but it did not matter, he knew the way easily. The floor plan was his, he had designed the extension installation before he closed the project, and the government had adopted the plans completely when they took over the facilities.

The door at the end of the hall was an extra thick one, but Pearson could hear the noise of the dolphins long before he reached it. As he opened the door, the noise grew so intensely that he thought for a moment that they were trying to communicate with him. He brushed the thought aside. Certainly, if they had something to tell him, they would have simply put the picture in his mind as Clickwhistle had. It did not occur to him that only Clickwhistle might be capable of such a thing.

The pool was a large one, and it too connected with an outside pool. Rathgall was just starting to raise the metal gate which separated the two pools as Pearson entered. The gate was halfway up before Pearson got close enough to be noticed.

Rathgall greeted him with a look of amused contempt.

"Come to see the solution of the problem?" he asked arrogantly. He cranked the gate up another three turns and the bottom of it cleared the water by a yard.

"I've got to get to Washington."

Rathgall frowned. "Come, come, Doctor, surely you haven't given up already." Hatred burned at him out of the tiny black eyes, a hatred seemingly as inexplicable as his own. Even if Pearson had evidence, Rathgall would not accept the idea that Pearson had spent the whole night communicating telepathically with dolphins. Yet he would need Rathgall's authorization to get a plane. "I must talk to His Excellency."

Rathgall smiled slyly. "A breakthrough already, Doctor? Surely, you haven't been working this early in the morning."

Four fins had passed under the gate before Pearson noticed them out of the corner of his eye, and even then their identity did not register until the sixth had passed through also. He could see five more circling in the pool outside. He turned away from Rathgall and stared in disbelief. "They're sharks!" he said.

Rathgall smiled acidly. "For once we are in agreement, Doctor."

"But you're putting them in the same pool with the dolphins!"

"An astute observation, Doctor," Rathgall said sarcastically. "It is my contention that the dolphin noises on that tape are a panic reaction caused by the presence of a large band of sharks."

Pearson stared at him in openmouthed disbelief. "You're crazy! Dolphins kill sharks!"

Rathgall snorted. "Surely, you don't believe that old wives' tale. Hardly a dolphin captured doesn't have scars on him from those creatures."

"If you lose a fight with a shark, you don't have scars! There's probably a dead shark for every scar."

"Ridiculous! They're terrified of sharks. They've been squealing ever since I started to raise the gate, which corroborates my thesis: the dolphins were panicked by a pack of sharks in feeding frenzy, and in their blind rush to escape, ran into the submarine."

"There were no sharks around!"

"Nonsense. Half of what were reported as whales were probably sharks, traveling with a whale shark which was misidentified as a killer whale."

"Whale sharks are vegetarians! They never travel with other sharks. That was a killer whale!"

The sharks swam cautiously at their end of the pool while the dolphins grouped themselves in a crescent around the two younger dolphins. The two smaller ones kept leaping out of the water almost in place and uttering shrill cries that seemed aimed more at Pearson than at the sharks. Pearson pointed at the sharks keeping a respectful distance. "I told you. The sharks won't even go near them."

Again that sly smile exposed Rathgall's shark teeth. "They will, once they've begun feeding frenzy. Once the blood in the water is thick enough, they'll attack anything that moves." He bent over and picked up one of three buckets of red liquid near the poolside. He poured the whole bucket into the water near the edge of the pool. The sharks converged on it instantly, slamming into each other in their rush, slashing their jaws like scythes.

Rathgall swung the second bucket in an underhand arc, splashing its contents out toward the center of the pool, spreading the pack out and giving it more room to maneuver. He splashed the third in a long arc toward the dolphins. The water roiled with slashing bodies as the sharks, crazed by the presence of so much blood, turned on each other, tearing away huge chunks of flesh with each pass.

The sharks began to spread out toward the dolphins' end of the pool, and the dolphins leaped from the water, whistling and shrilling. Pearson again had the feeling that they were trying to tell him something.

"As you can see," Rathgall nodded, "there will be no need for you to go anywhere, except back home. The mystery is solved; the government will simply have to look elsewhere for the cause of the trouble around *Dolphin Four*."

Two of the sharks streaked toward the dolphin end of the pool, but they were met before they got more than halfway by invisible punches that drove them almost up out of the water. Pearson knew they had been hit by dolphins, accelerating to thirty knots or better and slamming into the defenseless internal organs of the ribless sharks with their rock-hard beaks. Two more strikes like that and the skeletonless sharks would be dead, their vulnerable internal organs hemorrhaged beyond repair.

The sharks had scarcely settled back into the water when they were hit from the other side. One swam erratically back to the pack, while the other sank to the bottom. The first had not gone ten feet into the pack before he was torn apart by his fellow sharks. Rathgall watched the mounting frenzy of the sharks with a gleam in his eye.

Pearson watched nervously as part of the pack started to drift toward the center and then the far end of the pool. The dolphin whistling rose in intensity. Certainly, a dolphin could kill a shark, but whether those few dolphins could kill that many sharks even Pearson was not sure. The water near the edge still boiled with sharks.

"You see," Rathgall cried gleefully, "panic! Pure panic!" He laughed and moved back from the pool. Pearson had his back to the pool to talk to him. "It's imperative that I get to Washington. If you won't make the arrangements, I'll fly myself."

Rathgall stiffened. "I'm in charge of this project. You will do what I tell you to do and go where I tell you to go! And there will be no going to Washington! I'll do the reporting for this project, not *you!*" The larger man loomed closer to Pearson, trying to intimidate him with his bulk. Pearson took a short step back. "I *must* go to Washington! Don't you understand, I know what happened to *Dolphin Four!*"

Rathgall smiled, and the teeth appeared again. "Do you really?" he said menacingly. The teeth gave him away. Even before Clickwhistle relayed the message from the far end of the pool, Pearson knew. He was already moving as Rathgall plunged. Even Pearson was surprised at the quickness of his move as he threw him to the side, curving his upper body away like a dolphin evading the teeth of his only enemy. Rathgall's lunge carried him past Pearson, tangling his feet in the blood buckets and pitching him forward into the water. It might as well have been filled with piranhas.

When he looked, Pearson saw only the white-shirted arm emerge from among the fins. He had seen it all before.

CHAPTER THIRTY-TWO

It took him almost five minutes to get help, and by then there was too little left of Rathgall to be worth fighting the sharks for. The dolphins floated silently at their end of the pool, and the remaining sharks had passed back into the outer pool. He called for a plane while the Security officer was arriving, and then told for the fourth time how Dr. Rathgall had slipped on some blood at the edge of the pool and had fallen in.

As the Security officer took his deposition, he looked back toward the pool where one of the men with a boat hook had just pulled ashore a large chunk of meat swaddled in white cloth. The thought of how close he had come to being pushed into the pool made him shiver. The Security officer offered to finish questioning him later in the day, but Pearson refused, saying he would be in the capital filling in His Excellency later in the day. The mention of His Excellency seemed to shorten the questioning.

The helicopter was already at the Institute when he drove up. Baker and Fallow met him at the car with a barrage of questions. Pearson said only, "Rathgall's dead. The project's over. I want those two dolphins released immediately. Have them put back in the ocean exactly where they were caught, and make sure they get careful handling. I'll hold you personally responsible if anything happens to them," he said to Fallow.

"But what about the project?" Baker protested. "We won't be able to get other specimens for weeks."

"The project is over," Pearson said emphatically. "I want the other dolphins released also. Have it done today." He was climbing into the helicopter as he said the last words. The blades began to spin, and Baker and Fallow backed out of the way. Pearson leaned out and shouted over the noise, "I want those dolphins gone by tonight when I get back!"

He knew he would not get back. He knew it was the last time he would see either them or the Institute.

An hour later, he stepped into the conference room he had left the day before. The table was again full, and Kirby of the Internal Security Service stood as usual behind His Excellency's chair. He paused at the end of the table opposite His Excellency and waited. His Excellency nodded and Pearson began.

"Dr. Rathgall is dead, as you know. An exceptionally tragic loss because we had just made a breakthrough. Dr. Rathgall and I were in full agreement, for the first time in our careers, over the discoveries we had made in the first test. What we found out is truly mind boggling."

He paused and looked down the long table, stopping a second at each face. On the left side of the table, one small pair of eyes looked back at him alight with hatred; on the right, those eyes were joined by three more pairs. Behind His Excellency, another pair stared back hot with malice. Pearson shivered.

He had been about to tell them everything. He had been about to tell them how one extraterrestrial species in the shape of dolphins had destroyed the *Dolphin Four* to prevent another extraterrestrial species in the shape of killer whales from triggering the destruction of the earth. Five of the "men" in the room already knew everything he was going to say. He hoped they could not identify him as easily as he could them.

The pause in his speech grew awkward. He scrambled for words, for a new approach. "Dr. Rathgall and I were convinced," he said finally, "that we had found who had destroyed *Dolphin Four*. To prove our hypothesis and prevent the same thing from happening to the rest of the Dolphin System, I'll need *Dolphin Three* with a one-man crew, namely myself."

Kirby was howling with rage before Pearson had even finished his sentence, and the others took up the cry almost immediately. Even the humans in the group were opposed, the military men most of all. Admiral Hooker jumped to his feet in outrage. "Ridiculous! No civilian could operate—"

Pearson cut him off. "—a fully automated ship? Anyone with implanted hook-ups to the computer could sail that ship anywhere necessary for a limited time."

"But a command decision cannot be made by a civilian! *No* civilian has the capacity to . . ."

Pearson smiled and looked at His Excellency; the drumming of his index finger on the table was the only sign of his displeasure. The admiral missed both Pearson's smile and His Excellency's finger. "If you think I'm going to turn over a two billion . . ."

"'You'?!" His Excellency raised an eyebrow. His voice was like ice.

"I meant . . . Your Excellency, that . . . I . . . uh . . ." The admiral sat down abruptly.

Kirby interposed, leaning close from behind His Excellency. For a second, Pearson was afraid that the real power lay not *in* the chair but *behind* it. "What the admiral means, Your Excellency, is that an ordinary civilian is not capable of making the kind of instant de-

cisions that a military man or ruler is capable of making."
His Excellency's face did not change, but Kirby was too
close to the man's ear to see it. "*Dolphin Three* has the
means to trigger a global network of nuclear destruction.
Certainly, a mere scientist should not be trusted with
that kind of power."

"I don't want it," Pearson put in. "In fact, I want the
nuclear warheads disconnected immediately."

General Cobbitt flew up out of his chair like a killer
whale breaking the surface in some marine show, all
teeth and rage. "It would cripple the whole Dolphin
System! We'd have no Atlantic defense at all!" He turned
to His Excellency. "Your Excellency, we'd be powerless!
Helpless!"

Pearson shook his head vehemently. "*Dolphin One* and
Two have the same capability. Any of the four can
trigger any or all of the weapons in the system with just
a slight modification of trajectory." His Excellency
looked on impassively, and Pearson went on. "Your Excellency, there are only two choices now. Leave *Dolphin
Three* operable and have those warheads triggered
despite anything we do to stop them, or use *Dolphin
Three* as a decoy to contact the force that took over
Dolphin Four."

His Excellency smiled and nodded. "*Dolphin Three* became inoperable an hour after the attack. *Dolphin One*
and *Two* have crews standing beside the rocket to instantly defuse it if the hatch opens."

Kirby went white. His Excellency smiled without
looking at him. "Not everything, Kirby, is known to you."
He looked back to Pearson. "Do you know what the force
is?" he asked.

Pearson looked at him hard before replying. If the man
was not one of the killers, he was the closest thing the

planet had to equal them. And if he *was* one, Pearson was already dead. There was only one way to find out which he was. "No, sir, but I know it's not human."

His Excellency nodded. "Extraterrestrial?"

Pearson shrugged. "Possibly," he lied, "but I doubt it. You know that I've believed for a long time dolphins have a sufficient intelligence to match us in a thing like this; it may well be that they have always had other powers as well."

"You mean they could take over the controls of a vessel by telepathy," His Excellency said without surprise. Pearson was stunned. Obviously, His Excellency had heard the theory before, but who could have told him? Kirby and the others were not likely to have told him, and there was only one other group that knew. Pearson felt like a pawn again. The whole game of power going on around him made him dizzy. Every step he took seemed to have been planned a million centuries in advance. There had been no way anyone could have known what he was going to say—even he had not known—and yet someone seemed to know, and that someone could only be one of the other nine.

"Where would dolphins suddenly get such power?" His Excellency asked. Each question seemed a test to which His Excellency knew all the answers.

Pearson paused a moment, thought, and then nodded. "There were a number of unresponsive places when we mapped the dolphin brain, just as in humans, but a great many more in the cerebellum. I think the power resides there; I think dolphins have always had such powers, they just weren't ready to use them yet."

"Or perhaps we hadn't given them anything worth using it for," His Excellency added approvingly. "But then, the dolphin is man's unalterable friend." He was clearly mocking Pearson now, and Pearson understood why Rathgall had been made head of the project. Even his inclusion in the project seemed to have been a recommendation from someone. But whom? Certainly not Kirby, and Pearson doubted that there were many others whose advice was taken seriously.

"'Never in history,'" he quoted, "'has a dolphin attacked a man, even under the most extreme provocation.' Or so I've heard."

Pearson smiled ruefully as he searched for another lie. "When I wrote that, I thought it was true. I think it is still true for most dolphins, but we are, I believe, dealing here with a mutant form, *Delphinus superior,* if you will; a form only as related to the common dolphin as man is to the ape. A strain that we never had the chance to examine. With powers like that, it's unlikely that we would ever catch one without his wanting to be caught."

His Excellency smiled his cold smile again. He seemed to love having Pearson on the spot. Making people squirm was probably one of the few pleasures of his position. "That wouldn't make you much of an expert, would it?"

Pearson smiled too. "No," he said, "but I'm the best you've got left."

His Excellency shrugged deprecatingly. "You haven't told me anything I didn't already know."

"I can tell you how to stop them."

His Excellency's eyebrows raised infinitesimally. He looked inquiringly, not at Kirby, but at a small man with a melon-shaped forehead sitting at the end of the table near Pearson. The look seemed to imply that the man was somehow responsible for Pearson. Pearson looked at him closely. Behind his eye, there seemed to burn the same blue/green light that burned in Clickwhistle's.

The man gave a slight shrug as if to indicate that he

had no idea what Pearson was going to come up with, then turned attentively toward the scientist. He smiled a smile that sent a shiver down Pearson's spine. He shivered, not because it was the smile of a Kirby or a Cobbitt, but because it was a familiar smile, a fixed grin that was a hallmark, and it made him feel again a helpless tool in hands whose working he could not yet comprehend.

"I'll need *Dolphin Three*," he said.

"So you said," His Excellency noted, "but why *you?*"

"Because I've come closer than any man alive to communicating with a nonhuman who resembles them. When they communicate with us, we'll need someone there who has at least a vague understanding of their communication patterns."

His Excellency smiled as if Pearson had just said something foolish. "Why would they try to communicate with us?"

"To work out terms for a truce."

His Excellency's eyes shifted to the melon-headed man and back without satisfaction. "You seem to forget, Doctor, that we are no threat to them. By your own research, they are the fastest and most maneuverable creature in the sea. They're too quick to hunt in minisubs, and too maneuverable to hunt in anything larger. With their sonar superiority, we couldn't even find them. What terms could we possibly offer them?"

Pearson tried to think what his imaginary adversary would logically demand. "Their lives for ours, to begin with; after that, it will be up to you and the other world leaders to decide on the terms of the agreement. Maybe all they'll want is their ocean back, and an end to our pollution of it. Maybe they want even less. We've shared this planet with them for an awfully long time without confrontation; they must have some legitimate grievance you could straighten out with them. Maybe they'll demand our complete withdrawal from their territory; maybe they'll go halves on developing it. I don't know what they'll say, but I know you won't have anyone else who'll be able to translate when they do say it."

"Why should they want to communicate with us all of a sudden?"

"They've wanted to all along," Pearson answered. "Otherwise they wouldn't have armed the warhead."

His Excellency looked skeptical. "Look," Pearson went on, "we think of *Dolphin Four* as a Doomsday device. We think of it only in terms of an ultimate weapon. But, warheads were built into those missiles as a preliminary nonescalatory alternative."

The dolphin-headed man in gray nodded to His Excellency. "He's right, Your Excellency, those warheads were added because we saw the necessity for more alternatives than just massive nuclear retaliation. If they had intended to trigger the satellite system, they wouldn't have wasted time arming the warhead as well and giving us that much more time to block the launch. I believe Dr. Pearson is right that arming the warhead meant they were using our device as a warning, just as we intended to use it."

Cobbitt cut in. "I wouldn't call eight to twelve million dead a warning."

"What," Pearson asked, "would you have called it if we had fired it, General?"

"We wouldn't have fired it except in retaliation for a strike of theirs or for a direct invasion!"

His Excellency's man smiled his dolphin smile. "Perhaps that's why they did it."

Pearson went on. "I'd like the nuclear warhead disarmed but the satellite system left intact."

"That's taking a big chance if what you say is true," Admiral Hooker put in. "They could trigger the satellite system and that would be it."

"Perhaps, but it's a chance we have to take. They're not even sure we got their message. They'll have to try again. When they see the unarmable warhead, they'll know we understand. When they see the satellite triggering system still armed, they'll know we're trusting them, that we understand why they armed the first warhead and that we're ready to talk."

"But what if they really don't want to talk?" Kirby cut in. "What if all they wanted from the beginning was to obliterate us?"

The man in gray answered. "Quite frankly, gentlemen, if they had wanted to obliterate us, they would have. *But*, they only wanted to make a gesture."

Pearson picked up the clue. "We didn't stop that warhead—*they* did! And at a cost of a lot of their own lives. That missile was launched; the only way to stop it was to get their bodies in front of it, and they did that. Now, they could have let it go up and come down on one of the cities in our hemisphere, and they would have given us a good warning that they could use our own weaponry against us. But they didn't! They showed us our vulnerability without killing us. I don't think we'd have been so altruistic if the situation was reversed."

He could see the true humans around the table beginning to nod in reluctant agreement, and he went on. "Dolphins have taken a lot from man without striking back. A lot of what I did to dolphins by accident in the course of my experiments would have made me a war criminal if I had done it to my own species. But they didn't retaliate, and they haven't really retaliated yet. They've been incredibly forbearing with us, and I have a good idea that what they'll want from us may even be to our benefit in the long run."

His Excellency looked around the table for a rebuttal. Only Cobbitt had anything to say. "Even if it's true, I don't see why he couldn't just go along as one of the crew." His Excellency nodded thoughtfully and looked at Pearson for a reply.

"First of all, I believe they'll know I'm alone, just as they'll be able to perceive that the warhead is unarmed while the missile can still be fired. I think it's the kind of gesture they'll understand. Besides, you don't send your diplomats to the peace table with an armed guard, do you?" The general scowled at him, and the hatred burned furiously in his eyes. Pearson ignored it.

"Besides," he went on, "a crew could disconnect the satellite system. It looks too much like we're hedging our bet. I think we should play it straight and open with them, no tricks. Remember, there's nothing to stop them from firing *Dolphin One* and *Two* if they want to, unless we disarm them permanently. Do you want to disarm the *Dolphin System* now that you've made it your major line of defense, General?" Cobbitt shifted uncomfortably in his chair. Pearson shook his head.

"I think our enemies within our own species have too poor a record to trust for *that*, and I'm willing to bet that our new adversaries under the water will be far more trustworthy."

His Excellency turned part-way around in his chair and looked up at Kirby. The bulldog responded as if on command. "Sounds too farfetched to me."

"Does the spontaneous arming, aiming, and firing of a nuclear missile in a foolproof system sound any more probable to you?" Pearson cut in.

"Or would you prefer creatures from outer space as an

alternative?" Pearson laid heavy sarcasm on the second alternative as if the possibility were as preposterous as it sounded. It might not fool Kirby, but he had nothing to lose.

Kirby shrugged. "Well, even if the idea's right, I don't think we ought to trust them. It's too big a gamble." It was a feeble rebuttal, and Pearson knew that Kirby had fallen for it. His Excellency turned back to his man near Pearson. "How long to get him ready?"

The answer was immediate. "Three hours for the implantation of the control devices. About an hour intensive briefing. He can pick up the rest from the computer on board."

"All right, Pearson, it's yours." His Excellency nodded thoughtfully. "Perhaps your research will end up as a peaceful solution to things after all. Newman will take you where you need to go. Good luck."

Pearson smiled appreciatively. "Thank you, Your Excellency." Before he turned to go, he thought he saw a genuine smile on His Excellency's lips.

CHAPTER THIRTY-THREE

The captain of *Dolphin Three* frowned when he got the order to stop at Outpost Eleven to pick up an undisclosed personage. He considered himself at battle stations and cursed the civilian mind that could take a two-billion-dollar defense system that was all that stood between the Western Hemisphere and total annihilation and use it for a goddamned taxi.

He was not unaware that it was a similar stop that had cost *Dolphin Four* its existence, but he also knew that disobeying or even arguing with a decision signed by His Excellency himself would be more dangerous to him than a small thing like one of nukes going off under him. The second way only he would be dead; the other way everybody who had ever known him might perish.

He had been surprised to receive an order from His Excellency himself, and he had been surprised when he received the order to manually disarm and disconnect the warhead so that only a pair of human hands could arm it again. But he was even more surprised when his passenger came aboard and handed him the red envelope that identified him as acting directly in behalf of His Excellency.

If there was anything that a man carrying such an envelope could want in the Western Hemisphere and not get, Curry did not know what it was. If a man carrying that envelope commanded him to commit suicide, he would have thought twice before asking for an explanation. Still, he balked when the man gave him his order. In fact, he almost refused outright.

Pearson waited until the captain had had a chance to look over the red letter that was enclosed. It was headed "COSMIC CLEARANCE." Such a thing was of small moment to Pearson, who had had it, lost it, and had gotten it back again, but it was a personal tribute rather than a necessary privilege of rank to the captain. Pearson's tone was crisp and decisive. There was no doubt in the captain's mind that his visitor was a man who knew that the limits of his power were practically nonexistent.

"Captain Curry, you recognize the official despatch coding?"

"Yessir," Curry responded. He almost snapped into brace as he said it, despite himself. He had not felt so in awe of power since he was a cadet. "What are your orders, sir?"

"You will remove yourself and your crew immediately, Captain."

"Remove, sir?" Curry recognized the words, but he could imagine no reality that could fit them, and he assumed he had heard wrong.

"You will have ten minutes to gather your personal effects and remove your crew to the Outpost. You will be assigned there until further orders."

Curry stared at him openmouthed. It was as if someone had come up to him with a set of orders informing him that he had been dead for three weeks. It was incomprehensible. He stared at Pearson as if he had not heard a word and was still waiting for the stranger to give his first order.

Pearson leaned closer to him and looked at him oddly. "Are you listening, Captain?"

"Yessir!"

"Then why are you still standing there?"

"Sir?"

"Captain," he said in the measured tones of a man losing his patience, "you have only a little over nine minutes to gather your personal belongings and transport yourself and your crew to the Outpost."

"Yessir." The captain nodded briskly, but did not move.

Pearson subvocalized. There were no sounds in the room, but the computer relayed his words to the captain and the crew as well. The indirect route took only a fraction of a second longer than the direct route would have. "All hands will assemble their personal belongings and will report to the entrance hatch in eight minutes."

The captain seemed not to have heard that either, and Pearson snapped at him. "Are you listening, Captain Curry?" Curry nodded. "What have you been ordered to do?"

Curry spoke as if in a trance. "Get my personal belongings and abandon ship." He shook his head as if there were some hidden meaning in the words that he was obviously missing and which would add some lost sanity to his world.

Pearson shook his head; his tolerance for military men was not great at best. "Captain, that is a direct order under the authority of His Excellency himself. Are you refusing to obey it?"

Curry shook his head and stared blankly ahead. Either he had not heard it correctly or he had misunderstood it. But no matter how often he played it over in his head, it came out that he and his crew were having his vessel commandeered.

It was incomprehensible that this leprechaun should suddenly appear on board his ship with a red envelope and tell him to get off his own ship without even relieving him of his command. He would have been able to understand *that*, a simple message that he was being replaced as captain and that he would assist his replacement in any way he could and then depart to the capital. He had anticipated orders like that some day, when he was old enough to want to be kicked upstairs, but it was utterly impossible that it was happening to him now. And that he was being told to take his entire crew with him!

Pearson looked at the man sadly; he would have liked to explain it to him, but that was out of the question. He said softly, "Captain, I understand your feeling for your ship, but I have to get underway within ten minutes, and you are obstructing my schedule. Now, I would hate to have to get Security to remove you, but I will do so if necessary."

Curry turned and shuffled toward his desk. It held a steel box he hoped would be found if something happened to him, and he removed it mechanically. It took him only a little longer to gather up his uniforms and a set of civilian clothes and throw them into a bag. He took his own logbook, which he intended to turn into memoirs, if he could get them declassified. He left the other uniforms.

"I'll get the rest another time," he said as he shuffled past Pearson, saluting clumsily.

Pearson nodded and subvocalized. The computer did not pass the message on. "Position of crew?"

"ALL CREW MEMBERS ASSEMBLED AT 148.8 INTERNAL, EXCEPT CAPTAIN CURRY WHO IS AT 140.1 INTERNAL."

"Pipe party ashore and seal hatch. Then proceed to perimeter *Dolphin Four* blast area."

He sat down behind the captain's desk. It would take almost an hour to get there, and he had a few minutes to rest before he began his onboard briefing. Clickwhistle would meet him somewhere along the way. He was sure he would know the dolphin arrived.

He relaxed in the chair and let his head sink back into it. His head was still a little strange. He had not had a "residual" since he left the island, but he knew he would not return from the mission as surely as if he had already lived it.

He was headed east until Clickwhistle came along to tell him what to do next. He wondered what would happen to himself and Newman and the others who had given up their identity, their essence, to move like cogs in a big wheel that turned around Hummscreech's vision of the future that was already finished.

For the moment, he had that feeling of belonging again, of being a part of something larger and more significant than himself, and it made him long for that bubble world where he had floated at unity with himself and his brothers. It made him wish he had never awakened from Clickwhistle's vision. Deprivation of it was an agony, and he looked forward to the end of the mission.

He was still fifteen minutes from the rendezvous point when he felt the triumphant feeling of free fall riding alongside the vessel. He could hear/feel the echoes of the vessel as it slid through the water at well over a hundred knots, its own sonar making it almost blind beyond its stopping distance. Clickwhistle's own ranging sounds outraced the electronic pings of the ship's echolocation system.

Pearson felt the flow of the water go from laminar to turbulent and back again as Clickwhistle crossed the almost nonexistent wake of the ship. He rolled sideways and let himself slip back along the length of the ship toward the rear deck hatch, and coasted over it, examining it as they went.

Pearson ordered a stop short of the blast area and walked the hundred yards to the rear hatch missile chamber. He subvocalized the command to open the door, stifling the impulse to say "Open sesame!" just before it did. He stepped out onto the arming platform and picked up the two five-inch blocks of printed circuit that would complete the arming device. Turning the first on end, he opened the panel and checked the number of the grid against the number printed above the equally large slot in the warhead. The other four circuit grids were in place, but without a full set none of them was worth anything.

He turned the light side of the circuit grid so that it matched the light line that ran down the side of the left-hand slot. It slid in easily, and he felt it click into place. He picked up the second grid and did the same in the second row. When he pushed shut the curving white metal door, the missile was half armed. He went back out the door and down a flight to the next deck.

There he went through another door and stood on a similar platform below the one on which he had just stood. In front of him was another curved door that opened to a panel of numberless dials whose hands all rested to the far left of their ranges. He clicked three switches and closed the levers of two more circuits to arm the missile. When he had finished, he walked out of the door and started down the hall.

He could feel his beak banging at the catch on the outer hatch. He wriggled over the door and sped off to the side at a right angle to the long axis of the ship. At a hundred yards, he cocked his dorsal fin and glided into a tight turn. He concentrated his force on getting up speed; draining a little energy from the human pushed him up over a hundred and fifty knots.

It was a preliminary experiment to see if he could focus the enormous power that came from the mind of his lost brother. It was like grabbing the blade of a dynamo and then turning on the power, and the force slingshotted him ahead faster than he had dreamed.

The hatch fastened with a metal bar that had to be tilted backward to slide the hatch along its rails. Clickwhistle hit it full force with his beak. He was going faster than he had ever had to hit anything, and the concussion rattled his teeth. He was lucky not to break his lower jaw, but the job was done. When he had finished hitting it from the side, the metal lever bent almost double and remained immovable no matter what.

Pearson's head rang as well, and he had to stop and lean a hand on the wall until the spinning in his head stopped. He wondered what had happened; it was the first time he could remember the effects of an experience carrying over into his normal world. It was not a welcome experience, and his head still hurt when he got back to the Command Room.

Out of the box he had brought aboard with him, he removed three transparent cylinders, each with a coil of wire, and three argon lasers. He mounted them into a special bracket behind a double lens that focused all three beams as one and tightened the screws with a set of screw drivers from the box. When they were firmly in place, he mounted the whole thing onto a tripod.

Nowhere in the box was a power source, and nowhere on the ship were there facilities to connect one to the outside, so that the whole apparatus would not have frightened Kirby even if he had been able to find out about it. The tripod legs bent out at a ninety-degree angle about six inches from the bottom.

When he had finished securing them, he took out a plastic bag filled with bolts and a larger screw driver with a cowled head. The top of each screw had a place for a ratchet attachment. He taped the bag of screws and the ratchet to one leg of the tripod, picked up the whole thing, and carried it down to the decompression chamber.

In a few minutes, he was suited up and outside, swimming along the side of the ship, dragging the laser in its plastic sack. When he reached the deck just behind the hatch, he felt for the raised clips into which each leg of the tripod was meant to fit. During inspections, the main unit of the stress-testing device was mounted there. It was on the tripod for this machine that Pearson had mounted the lasers with their special protective bracket.

He slid a leg into each of the slots and unstrapped the bag. He took out the ratchet handle and one screw at a time. He tightened the screw as much as possible by hand and then fitted the ratchet into the head and turned. In another minute and a half, he had tightened all three to his satisfaction.

He had almost finished before he saw the other dolphin. He had seen Clickwhistle overhead immediately, but he had not noticed the other one. It was a dolphin like none he had ever seen before. The way the jaw jutted forward and the flat style of his float made him seem more like a barracuda than a dolphin.

Where Clickwhistle bobbed like a small boy expecting a parade, Longscreech hung poised like a spear. The dolphin twirled his right eye out and down and stared at Pearson. Pearson almost shivered. If any dolphin could attack a man, that was the one, and if His Excellency had a counterpart among the dolphins, Longscreech was it.

From time to time, he would slap his tail sideways, without moving himself very far forward or backward. He seemed like a boxer jabbing at his shadow. He would thrash his head in the same way, practicing as well. The presence of the other dolphin reminded him that he was just a small part in a puzzle well beyond his understanding, and it made him uncomfortable.

Clickwhistle came and nudged him back toward the entrance. He swam toward it, pausing only once to look back over his shoulder at the form that hovered over the ship like an avenging demon sent to guard it.

Once inside, he made his way to the Command Room and told the computer to turn on the outside monitor. Clickwhistle floated next to the laser, while in the upper left-hand corner of the picture hung the black torpedo of Longscreech. Even knowing what their weapon was, it would have been difficult to say which was the more dangerous.

Clickwhistle floated at a ninety-degree angle to the long axis of the ship. With his right flipper, he worked the laser steadily through the 360-degree ball of its motion. He had the urge to fire it, but he knew there would be no whales if he did. Instead, he contented himself with working it through its ranges, sighting and following targets no one else could see.

Clickwhistle opened his mouth slightly and pressed his tongue up against the horny beak of his mouth, letting the salt water run through and over the exquisitely sensitive taste buds on both surfaces. Far more sensitive than a dog's nose, the dolphin's tongue detected the first faint hint of the coming enemy. They were coming in from all sides at once, and when they arrived, the dolphins would be surrounded.

Longscreech's sonar detected them long before the ship's equipment had any inkling that there was something coming. He tensed in a peculiarly undolphin way, and swam a little to the side, as if to be in motion when he crossed his original position again. Clickwhistle hung near the laser, keeping his delicate skin away from the abrasive metal. Pearson had been sent back inside so he would not have to use up a large portion of his brain with the trivia related to survival in the alien environment of the water.

Clickwhistle detected the whales almost as quickly as Longscreech, and he edged around the controls of the laser cannon. The gun had three times the breadth of the best phased laser, and while its power would put the killers out of the body for a while, it would not destroy them utterly. At least not in its present state. But Clickwhistle had made its present state no more its true state than an unarmed bomb is an armed one. For the moment, it stood as only a triple-barreled laser cannon, deadly enough in short term, but nothing that would frighten their enemies.

The whales closed from all directions, moving at top speed. They had been almost half a mile apart when Clickwhistle had first detected them; if they kept speed and formation, they would be less than twenty yards apart when they were close enough to make their attack on the vessel. Clickwhistle and Longscreech had avoided any communication for hours before so that they could not be detected. They felt the brain waves of the whales as they drew closer, the giveaway that usually foiled a sneak attack. Only by blanking their minds could they pull off the surprise they had done at the Great Massacre of Hummscreech's birth.

They were not masking their brain waves now, and Clickwhistle knew it meant they were either unaware of or unconcerned with the presence of him and Long-screech. It meant they were coming all at once, to trigger the bomb, coming in mass in case there was any interference and also to leap from their forms to pursue their old enemies when they fled the doomed planet. Only those whose form was destroyed before they could leave it would be unable to give chase, and they were ready to make those sacrifices.

Clickwhistle could detect eighteen of them, one every twenty degrees around the clock. It was going to be tight.

CHAPTER THIRTY-FOUR

Clickwhistle waited until they were within sonar contact of the submarine and easily within his sonar range before he threw the wraps off his presence. He entered Pearson's mind with a rush of taste, sound, and sight of the approaching enemy. He let it seep deep into Pearson's unconscious and with it the shattering of the old world/organism and the eons of pursuit. He waited for the rush of rage it would trigger. What he got was rage interspersed with an even greater intensity of energy in the form of longing.

Clickwhistle swiveled the laser to port in a short sweep. His mind acted as a prism, focusing the energy from Pearson's mind through his own and into the gun in the same fashion the killer whales had turned their own brain waves into electrical waves to fire the missile. The energy emitted was astounding, far more than even Clickwhistle had anticipated, and it took all his strength to channel it into the gun.

The crystals glowed and flared as the light passed up and down the tube and through the crystal at the end that made their light coherent. The six-inch beam of light that shot from the front of the gun carried enough energy to melt lead. The beam sizzled through the water, vaporizing the water in front of it so rapidly that it created a vacuum in its wake. Clickwhistle swung the gun in a wide arc, following it around the circle with his body.

The whales had slowed their swimming as soon as they had sensed the change in the presence of the dolphin. That there were only two of them had made them more cautious still, and they were ready for some kind of evasive action before Clickwhistle had even begun to open up. He began the sweep of the laser at three o'clock and swept counterclockwise toward twelve. The first ninety degrees of his sweep netted him four kills and one probable.

The laser cut a swath six inches wide through water and flesh alike. The first of the ten-ton monsters had caught the beam across his teeth from right to left. It sectioned him longitudinally, separating the long halves of him by a six-inch layer of vaporized water, flesh, blubber, and bone. The suction of the vacuum created by the laser's beam pulled the two halves together, but almost before they hit, they had begun to slide off one another like top and bottom halves of some incredible sandwich.

The second had been caught in the same fashion, though the beam had struck him above the mouth and had sliced him as neatly as a giant sword. The third had begun to dive, and the beam caught him transversely a few feet ahead of his huge, triangular dorsal fin. The bottom half of him skidded downward as if dropped by the upper half, which thrashed a moment before following its bottom half to the bottom as well.

The fourth had veered to the side and presented a lateral view to the beam, which continued its arc through the water as if it had come into contact with nothing. Turning sideways had saved it only a fraction of a second of life, but it had given the whale enough time to cry out and warn the others.

The whale next to it had thrown itself violently upward in a grotesque question mark, but it was too slow, and the beam truncated it six feet above the flukes. The tail fell away like a first stage separating from a climbing rocket, and it struggled erratically upward on its flippers alone toward the air.

The rest of the circle had dispersed up and down randomly, and Clickwhistle had wheeled around 180 degrees from where he had started before he hit another. He had begun to move the gun not merely in a circle but in a rising and falling wave, the amplitude of which caught one more of the whales across its white belly just above the flippers. The beam passed through lung and bone like a giant razor, and the big mammal separated into two uneven pieces.

Clickwhistle accompanied his turn with a continuous creaking-door series of clicks and supersonic whistles. The first series caught the more distant objects, and the second brought his body an instantaneous location of the closer ones. His cries hit and echoed from the massive bodies undulating toward him, and seemed to light them up for him like targets on a pinball machine.

From nine o'clock to six, he found the range again; the quickness of the whales was no match for his instant echolocation and the quicker maneuverability of the gun on its tripod swivel. The beam cut an irregular path across the bodies of three of the attackers, leaving them clacking their teeth in rage as the life flowed out of their severed tails. In two others, the beam slashed through the black skin of their foreheads, severing their brains like so much packed butter.

There was no impact, as there might have been from a torpedo or a shell, to knock them backwards, and no explosion to throw them one way or another. The beam merely sizzled through the water, segmenting them into dead or dying fractions of themselves. They were not blown away, or knocked back, and most seemed to glide ahead a few yards and then simply run out of power and glide down to harder landings on the bottom.

Only the shrilling of the two dolphins and the whales' screams of rage and pain made any sound at all. The sizzle of the water behind the beam of Clickwhistle's weapon made less noise than the swinging blade of a broadsword, and the slow-motion, sometimes erratic, fall of its victims made the whole scene seem more an underwater ballet than a battle.

Clickwhistle swung the gun into the fourth quadrant of the circle before he was firing it at point-blank range. The beam traveled less between hits, and there was less need to maneuver it up and down. The bodies of two whales dropped short of the ship, and half the lower jaw and an attached three tons of body slammed into the hull below and to the right of where Clickwhistle spun in his circle. His back was to the original direction of his firing when the first of the whales came close enough to tear him free of the gun.

It fell only inches short, and that because it dove with its huge mouth open to grasp and rake the dolphin. Long-screech had already passed his earlier station in full flight, his avidity churning his body forward at over a hundred knots. His jutted lower jaw welded to his upper one with a hundred interlocking, conical teeth made him into a nine-hundred-pound spear traveling faster than a human-made torpedo. Though he weighed less than a twentieth of his huger adversary, his blows were as deadly as theirs.

The whale had opened his mouth for a death bite of Clickwhistle when Longscreech hit him. The dolphin's hard, bony beak struck him on the side of the jaw, just at the end of the crack of the mouth, dislocating the mandible and knocking the huge animal a foot off its prey. The impact jarred Longscreech, but it did not dampen his ardor for the attack. He turned in a short circle like a karate master and lunged with almost equal force under the jaw of a second whale. His beak hit the softer layer of fat and muscle between the horseshoe of bone that made up the lower jaw.

The blow slammed the mouth of the huge whale closed, jarring its teeth, splitting the skin, and tearing at the bottom of the tongue. Longscreech ricocheted from the impact downward, and with a powerful flap of his tail, shot himself upward into the stomach of another whale. His impact bruised the whale's lungs and drove him a few inches off his mark so that his teeth snapped harmlessly to the side of Clickwhistle.

With four rapid strokes of his tail, Longscreech shot himself to the surface and through the interface into the air. A sharp expiration/inspiration sucked in a lungful of air. He entered the water again with a full six minutes' worth of air, and none too soon. His re-entry carried him into a diagonal dive that allowed him to strike the back of one of the whales who had missed Clickwhistle on the first pass.

The hard beak hit him like a kidney punch behind the dorsal fin, and the huge jaws swung like a crane toward the dolphin. The six-inch teeth slashed the water just ahead of Longscreech's flipper as he threw himself into a tight turn around full, and down under the beast. The gyre of his descent, like the concentric spiral of a landing plane, carried him almost into the path of the laser, and the water sizzled a few feet in front of his face.

Clickwhistle himself was short on air, though he had expended less of his reserve than Longscreech in swinging the gun. Clickwhistle felt the strain like a sprinter. His mind ached with the strain of collecting Pearson's energy and focusing it while calculating the angles of fire and positions of his targets, and swimming in a circle at the same time to swing the gun.

When the gun again hit three o'clock, Clickwhistle swung it back again toward six, splitting the tail section of one of the whales as Longscreech knocked it aside. The beam caught it along the genital slit and elegantly cut its long, thick tail and peduncle into a pair of legs on which it would never walk and very little longer swim.

The behemoth shuddered past and dropped away toward the bow of the ship. Clickwhistle caught one so close that the beam burned a single hole entirely through it from nose to tail. Its momentum carried it almost into the laser, and it hit Clickwhistle with the side of its huge head as it slid by. A spasmodic slap of its flipper as it passed knocked Clickwhistle away from the gun and sent him sprawling toward the rear of the vessel.

Had the next whale thought to ram the gun instead of trying to gut Clickwhistle, the battle would have been over. But the monster was coming in from the second quadrant and was closer to Clickwhistle than the gun and so snapped at the body that wriggled away just outside the snap of the jaws.

Clickwhistle did a sharp turn to his right and made a tight circle that drew him behind his pursuer. Before the huge whale could cut to his left, Clickwhistle was back at the gun and had turned it on his pursuer. The beam cut across the face and extended in the same fashion through the whole body, vaporizing nearly a half ton of flesh. The whale gave a spasm and glided downward.

Only one of the attackers remembered the hatch, and that one had seen the bent handle that kept it from opening. That one rammed it with all his ten tons, snapping it off at the base and freeing the hatch cover. He was in the process of pushing the hatch open with his head when Clickwhistle saw him.

The body of the killer angled up and away at forty-five degrees from the ship, and the beam came in and down as Clickwhistle regained control of it. It cut into the side of the dorsal fin and continued in and down through the center of the head, slicing off a three-ton slab of flesh. An avalanche of blubber and muscle sloughed off toward the bottom. The rest of the body toppled to the left and slammed into the bottom just a few yards past the side of *Dolphin Three*.

The rest of the whales had dispersed, and Clickwhistle got no more than a faint echo of them before he burst for the surface and a gulp of air.

CHAPTER THIRTY-FIVE

Clickwhistle did not break the surface in a great leap as Longscreech had. His short arc carried him immediately back down to the gun with a full supply of air. The short maneuver was a well-needed respite for his mind, and he felt free of a thousand-ton weight as he let go of Pearson's mind on his upward climb. When he returned, he found that he had to keep himself motionless near the hull of the ship before he could maintain contact again.

Longscreech dropped in a short spiral to a position only a few yards above Clickwhistle. He seemed to lean forward in the water as if anxious for the next attack. One of his delicate flukes was badly torn, and there was a long, jagged tear along his side from which the blubber sealant extruded in long, thick strands like ribbons. Clickwhistle knew by the thickness and number of the strands that the wound was deep, probably a mortal one, and that Longscreech's hunger for more contact was because the next blow would probably be his last. No more than three of the whales remained.

Longscreech turned himself slowly in the opposite direction of Clickwhistle and sent out both his short- and long-range sounds. Clickwhistle did likewise and tightened his grasp on Pearson's mind. Less than a half mile away, three single outlines were discernible to them, but hardly more than a mile and a half farther, echoes returned from fifty more. The three whales turned and fitted themselves into the pattern of the attack as it swam past. Clickwhistle let the image burn into Pearson's mind.

The killer whales were less than a quarter mile away when Pearson gave the signal. They were far enough within the blast area to make escape impossible. Clickwhistle held Pearson's mind like a small bird huddling in a man's hand. He neither controlled it, nor had he broken contact; he simply waited for the surge of power that he knew was sure to come. At the farthest curve of the world, on the far side of the planet from the force that waited for them to break cover, the Self waited also.

Almost unaware of what was happening except for a report from one dolphin stationed outside the battle area, the Self waited for the signal Hummscreech knew would come.

They waited patiently to make their break in a straight line out from the planet—on the opposite side from the force waiting for them to burst up out of the surface and scatter like hunted fish in all directions. They would, at the speed of light, burst from the planet just ahead of the pursuit they had evaded for so many, many eons. That was the way it went, that was the way it had already happened. That was the fate they were destined this time to play out. Countless light-centuries ahead they would come bursting back into that water, tail first, traveling in the opposite direction but no less certain of its inevitability than they were to be traveling outward this time.

But that was a whole expiration of the universe away, and there was still a long, long time of going outward before they could come back. They had paused long enough, indulged themselves long enough; they had held back the inevitable flow of all things outward toward the ultimate dispersal and the inevitable contraction.

The time was almost upon them, and they could hear as clearly as Clickwhistle while Pearson gave the command. He spoke it aloud, and the computer automatically made the announcement as if there had actually been a crew on board. The words rang through the suddenly empty chamber in which Pearson sat. "Fire missile one."

The computer began to countermand the order as Clickwhistle probed its mechanism and burned out its wires. It was his mind and not the computer that activated the firing mechanism of the missile, but it had to seem to be done through the computer for the illusion that he had triggered his own death to be credible to Pearson.

Clickwhistle and the rest waited for the burst of energy that no dolphin, with his understanding of the way of the universe, could generate. They waited for the agonized horror and panic that only a dolphin mind so long human that it had grown wild and uncontrollable and had forgotten the nature of the game could produce. Only the absolute and unmitigated terror of death could give them the energy they needed to make their escape.

Clickwhistle fed back to Pearson the computer's reply: "MISSILE ARMED AND FIRING." Then he let seep through the picture he could see of the hatch, still three quarters shut, despite the futile efforts of the killer whale.

The whales were almost on top of them; Clickwhistle could see their black and white mountains of flesh streaking toward him, but he held the picture from Pearson. To die in company of his enemies would lessen the impact of the event, and they could not afford that. There was little time left as he aimed the laser.

Pearson sat in the Command Room, a cold sweat beginning on his forehead. The missile was fired, the bullet on its way to his brain. He tried to tell himself that a universe with creatures like the Self could not possibly end; he tried to tell himself that there was another life waiting for him behind, but it was no good, that was a dolphin knowledge and he was dying a human death.

All he could see before him was the eternal, black emptiness of his death. He could feel the slight shudder as the missile lifted off, followed instantaneously by the impact and detonation against the hatch. As it hit, he screamed his "No!" to death.

The whales had almost closed the circle, still moving at full speed. They had come in like a battalion of kamikazes, expecting mostly to perish in the attempt but sure that one of them would get through, and one would be all that was needed. They had not even taken evasive action and expected the beam to zing toward them at any second.

They closed to within a few body lengths of the vessel as the torrent of life force poured itself into Clickwhistle's mind and, through it as through a prism, into the laser and out again—but *not* into the closing circle of whales.

As the beam of the laser passed above them and out over the curve of the world, the first of the whales guessed its destination, but it was too late to prevent or warn against it. The howl of Pearson's terror and his longing for life shot the beam out over the edge of the world and into space, burning itself directly into the creature and driving it back, as a figure trapped in the stream of a fire hose is driven back, and knocked down, and, though able to rise again unhurt, is for the moment helplessly pushed back by the force.

There was only a second between the burst of energy and the detonation of the warhead against the hatchway door, but an instant in human time was more than enough for the power that burst so unexpectedly from the planet to dazzle, daze, and bewilder the force that waited halfway to the Coal Nebulae like an invisible cloud for the escape of the Self.

A second was far more than enough for the Self to take their head start out between the stars again, into the dark crevices of the universe farther from the unity of their original home, on the run again and one step ahead of the force that sought their utter annihilation. But one step was enough, and it would always be enough until it was time for the Self and the life force to turn around and begin the long drive back again toward the unity that was the universe in its original form.

The force that trailed them would be slower now, weaker by all the parts of itself that had been driven not merely out of the body but out of existence by the nuclear explosion that had boiled a cubic mile of ocean in the mid-Atlantic.

Near the far curve of the planet's surface, a thousand dolphins became no more than clever mammals again. Half the planet away, fifty-three killer whales and fifty-three more parts of a larger organism ceased to exist until the universe had reversed itself and worked its way back to that point again. At the same spot, the body of a man and two dolphins were equally obliterated, but the forces that had inhabited them were long gone.

Pearson felt himself a part of the Self again; he felt before him the dark, cold places between the stars, and he knew the long, long flight that loomed ahead and the dark, dreadful, inexorable pursuit that would soon assemble itself again behind. But none of it mattered to him.

No longer were there separate parts, no longer a Clickwhistle and a Longscreech, a Longwhistle and a Hummscreech, a Pearson and a Cathy; but only one entity now, again one single form and being until the next stopover and the next game of cat and mouse between the forces of death and the forces of life. A billion more games of hide-and-seek away, things would reverse themselves and the chased would become the chaser. A million billion games from now, it would all re-form and the Self would be together again. For the moment, Pearson was on his way home.